PRINCESS OF THE WILD SEA

Megan Frazer Blakemore

BLOOMSBURY
CHILDREN'S BOOKS
NEW YORK LONDON OXFORD NEW DELHI SYDNEY

BLOOMSBURY CHILDREN'S BOOKS
Bloomsbury Publishing Inc., part of Bloomsbury Publishing Plc
1385 Broadway, New York, NY 10018

BLOOMSBURY, BLOOMSBURY CHILDREN'S BOOKS, and the Diana logo are trademarks of
Bloomsbury Publishing Plc

First published in the United States of America in January 2023
by Bloomsbury Children's Books

Bloomsbury books may be purchased for business or promotional use. For information on bulk
purchases please contact Macmillan Corporate and Premium Sales Department at
specialmarkets@macmillan.com

Library of Congress Cataloging-in-Publication Data
Names: Blakemore, Megan Frazer, author.
Title: Princess of the wild sea / Megan Frazer Blakemore.
Description: New York : Bloomsbury Children's Books, 2023.
Audience: Ages 8–11. | Audience: Grades 4–6
Summary: Cursed Princess Harbor Rose lives on a remote island
as she waits for a hero to sweep her away, but when a foe rooted
in dark magic threatens her beloved island, Harbor
Rose must find a way to call the hero before time runs out.
Identifiers: LCCN 2022027906 (print) | LCCN 2022027907 (ebook)
ISBN 978-1-5476-0956-7 (hardcover) | ISBN 978-1-5476-0957-4 (ebook)
Subjects: CYAC: Blessing and cursing—Fiction. | Princesses—Fiction.
Magic—Fiction. | Islands—Fiction.
Classification: LCC PZ7.B574 Pr 2023 (print) | LCC PZ7.B574 (ebook) |
DDC [Fic]—dc23
LC record available at https://lccn.loc.gov/2022027906
LC ebook record available at https://lccn.loc.gov/2022027907

Book design by Yelena Safronova
Typeset by Westchester Publishing Services
Printed and bound in the U.S.A.
2 4 6 8 10 9 7 5 3 1

To find out more about our authors and books visit www.bloomsbury.com
and sign up for our newsletters.

For Dad,
who loves the sea and telling stories

PRINCESS
OF THE
WILD SEA

PART ONE

CHAPTER ONE

Three days after Harbor Rose turned twelve, a boy washed up on the shore of Small Island. While many things had washed up there, only once before had a child.

The day of Harbor's birthday started off typically enough. Harbor ran down the hill from her cottage to The Place Where Things Wash Up hoping to beat Mr. Coffin, but he was already there. He waded in the water where it lapped at the small beach. His pants were rolled up to his calves, his blue shirt neatly tucked in, and his straw hat was pressed firmly onto his head. He held a basket brimming with treasures.

Harbor scowled. "Good morning, Mr. Coffin."

Each morning the two hurried to The Place Where Things Wash Up. Whoever got there first got first dibs.

Mr. Coffin reached his hand into the water and pulled out something black and rectangular. He turned it over in his hand. There was a hinge at one end and a seam all around. Carefully, he unfolded it. The bottom half was an array of buttons, each with a single number. The top was a gray bit of glass.

"What you got there?" she asked.

Without looking up, Mr. Coffin said, "I don't need some freckle-faced girl taking my things."

She brushed her fingers over her cheeks, which were, in fact, freckled. Her sun-blonde hair whipped into her mouth.

"Is it an adding machine?" she asked.

"Hmm," he said.

"Does it work? Can you turn it on? Let me see," she begged, stepping into the water to get a better look.

He dropped it into his basket. "It is none of your concern."

Harbor wanted to tell him that, as a princess, everything was of her concern, but she knew Mr. Coffin would only laugh. She was a princess, but no one treated her like one.

Small Island was part of The Lands of Lapistyr. In her more melodramatic moments, Harbor described herself as an exiled princess. She would flop onto the ground, throw her arm over her forehead, and proclaim, "I am banish-ed!" She was not, in fact, banished. She was simply away from her homelands for a time—for her own safety.

Mr. Coffin splashed farther into the water.

"Can I just see it?" she asked.

Mr. Coffin stood up straight. "You are like a cat," he told her. "And your curiosity will surely be the death of us all."

4

Mr. Coffin was prone to his own bouts of melodrama.

She couldn't get her mind off that strange little black box. Mr. Coffin's unwillingness to share it made her even more set on seeing it. "Mr. Coffin, do you know what today is?"

"Tuesday."

"No," she said. "Well, yes. But it's also my birthday, and since it's my birthday maybe you could—" But as she spoke, Mr. Coffin's face did something funny. It tightened and softened at the same time, like it was at war with itself.

"I know." His voice, too, battled itself, soft and hard, rough and smooth.

Maybe he was mad because he didn't want to be on Small Island. Maybe he was mad about having been sent there from Lapistyr and her birthday only reminded him of how angry he was about it. "Only one more year," Harbor said. "Then I'll be safe and we can go back to Lapistyr." Mr. Coffin set his jaw in stony silence.

Harbor retreated to an old boat that had washed up on the shore ages ago. Its hull pointed skyward, and she climbed on top where she absentmindedly played with the necklace her mother had given her when they'd first left the royal palace. It had a tiny glass globe for a charm, filled with sand from Lapistyr. She liked to rub the globe with her fingers as she thought. She stared out over the water that rippled and glowed pink in the morning sun. She felt that sun reach onto her toes, then her legs, then right up onto her face. Mr. Coffin grunted and groaned as he picked up and examined each item.

The ocean stretched for miles and miles and, as far as Harbor could tell, never stopped. It had to stop somewhere, though. She had long ago reasoned this. If things like mixing bowls and bicycle wheels had not been made on the island, and hadn't been brought from Lapistyr, there had to be a Somewhere Else where they had been made. Harbor didn't know where that Somewhere Else was or what it was like. They mixed ingredients there, she assumed. And rode bicycles there and poured water from pitchers. They clipped things into their hair, played with dolls and toy cars. These were things she could surmise, and still it was not a complete picture. When she returned to Lapistyr, perhaps she would learn more. Perhaps her father would even bring her there someday.

"There," Mr. Coffin said, having put one last item into his basket: a green mug with a stenciled image of a woman in a crown. It was quite lovely, and Harbor was momentarily jealous. She imagined tea would taste very good out of that mug, and anyway her family were the royal ones. Shouldn't they have the royal mug? Mr. Coffin took his basket by the handle and carried it up the path toward the village.

"Goodbye, Mr. Coffin," Harbor called after him.

As soon as he was around the bend, Harbor jumped from the rock and began her own search of the beach. She found a small toy elephant with its head on a spring, so it bobbled back and forth when she touched it. Next, she found a broken necklace chain and a shard of blue-and-white pottery.

Satisfied with her haul, Harbor walked up the path, pockets full of treasures.

The sun had risen on her twelfth birthday. She was another year older. This was the year, she was quite certain, she would finally get her magic.

CHAPTER TWO

Harbor thought of her curse often, but especially on her birthdays. Her mother and aunts had told her the story so many times it felt like a tale about somebody else.

Once upon a time, on a beautiful island, there lived a queen and a king. The queen and king were kind, generous, and full of laughter. They ruled their lands with benevolence, and their leadership was admired throughout the realm. Peace reigned. The queen and king wanted for nothing, except for a child. Years went by and their longing grew greater. Eventually, on a beautiful summer morning, a child was born. The queen and king named their daughter Harbor Rose. Harbor because, as the next queen, she represented safety and prosperity, and Rose for the glow of her cheeks. All agreed she was the loveliest child ever to have been born on Lapistyr with hair like honey, eyes that sparkled, and rolls of fat perfect for squeezing. Not that anyone squeezed a princess.

The christening was the largest party Lapistyr had ever seen. Representatives from lands near and far came to give the child their gifts. The Ice Kingdom of the north brought furs for the child to sleep in. The Soth of the south brought an intricate trellis made of steel for roses to climb. The free people of the small islands gave canoes and hammocks. The woodworkers of Benspeir, the mountaintop homeland of the king, sent a hand-carved cradle, though of course they did not come themselves. The blacksmiths and the glass-blowers of Lapistyr worked together to create a window for her royal bedroom with a map of the island, her glowing crown at the center of it. Gardeners brought bouquets of flowers and planted climbing roses beneath her window.

Harbor was dressed in a gown of pale green, trimmed with the stones of her aunts: sapphires, rubies, opals, pearls, and amethysts. Mica was used like sequins on her train, and a small crown of coral rested on her head. These aunts were invited from far and wide. All but one, who was presumed to be wandering in The Somewhere Else.

After the feast, but before the dancing, it was time for the aunts to give their blessings.

First came the eldest sister, Sapphire, a Seer who gave the child the gift of courage:

Though storms may come and darken the sea,
True courage will descend on thee.
Birds fly high, and seals dive low.
You will see which way to go.

The crowd murmured. If the Seer thought the girl needed courage, what might that portend?

Opal Pearl came next. She was the second eldest. It was assumed that, as a Protector, Opal Pearl would give the princess a protection blessing. Instead, she bestowed the gift of creativity:

Each periwinkle contains a spiral,
Each oyster makes a pearl.
Your mind creates a tapestry,
To reflect our little world.

Ruby, a Healer, next approached the child. Her blessing was a simple but essential one. She gifted the child good sense:

Needle, comb, leaf, branch,
Trees reach for the sky.
Good sense you need, my darling child,
For you were meant to fly.

Finally, the turn came to Amethyst, the youngest. Amethyst was a Shifter, but she was known for using her magic in frivolous ways. She picked up the child and cradled the baby to her chest, whispering soft words into her ear. Before she could bestow her gift, the doors of the hall crashed open.

It was Micah, the aunt thought to be wandering away in The Somewhere Else. She swung her shimmering gray cape off her shoulders and let it fall. A footman grabbed it before it touched the ground.

"I see there is some civility left in these lands," Micah announced.

Under her cape she wore a mishmash of clothes, nothing suitable to a royal party: a long, ruffled skirt over denim pants and work boots. Her hair was tied up in a bun laced through with ribbons and string.

The queen jumped to her feet. "Micah!" she exclaimed. "We had heard you had left the realm."

"So you heard, and so I had—for a time."

She strode across the room toward the child. Amethyst clutched the baby to her chest.

"Amethyst, my dear," Micah said to her. "You fear your sister?"

Amethyst said nothing, but she set her feet more firmly.

"You should all be afeared!" Micah announced, spinning around with her hands held wide. "A war is coming!"

"Micah, we apologize for the oversight," King Ash said. His brown eyes showed fear, something the citizens had never seen. "We shall set a place for you. Please, join us."

"There is no time for parties, no space for joy," Micah replied. "Child, here is my blessing," she said. But what she delivered, all knew was a curse:

Before you reach age thirteen,
With languid limbs and eyes of green,

Something strange, something new,
You'll prick your skin as bright as dew.
A single drop of blood will fall,
A single tear you'll shed.
And by the time the tears have dried,
You may all be dead.

"Stop!" Sapphire ordered.

"Why must you curse our child?" the queen cried.

"It is not I who have cursed her; it is you." She stared at the queen and king, and her eyes narrowed at her sister's husband. "Your enemy is coming. I have seen it. It shall lay waste to the land and make it barren. Consider this your warning. It is more than you deserve." With that, she snatched her cape from the footman and left the hall.

All were silent.

Even the baby, who looked at Amethyst with wide eyes.

"Sweet child," said Amethyst. "I have not yet given you my gift." She placed the child back in her cradle. "I cannot undo the curse that Micah has done." The crowd murmured. Were their fates truly tied to this young and undisciplined sister? Amethyst held up her hand. "No, I cannot change the curse, but I can soften it." She took a deep breath, thought for a moment, then gave her blessing:

A drop of blood, sleep will descend,
A hero rises to bring war's end,

A stranger comes from far away,
Fights death and brings a golden day.

Amethyst's blessing was the best it could be, but, it must be noted, it did not hold off the enemy. It promised sleep instead of death but didn't keep the child out of danger. "If we protect her, no harm will come to her," Sapphire said. "And no war shall come to our lands."

"But how shall we protect her?" the queen begged.

"We hide her," said Opal Pearl. "We hide us all."

CHAPTER THREE

Harbor Rose's shingled cottage listed to one side when the wind blew from the north. When the wind blew from the west, it nearly touched its toes. But when the wind blew from the east, up the cliff and against the rattly windows, the cottage stood tall and steady as a lighthouse.

Harbor pushed open the side door and stepped into her kitchen where her mother, Queen Coralie, was at the stove, frying up eggs from the chickens out back. Harbor's aunt, Ruby, sat at the table with a mortar and pestle, grinding herbs to make tea.

"Ruby!" Harbor cried. Ruby wasn't a stranger to the cottage, but it was always a pleasant surprise to see her.

"Good morning, birthday princess," Ruby said.

"How was Mr. Coffin this morning?" her mother asked.

Harbor scowled. "He got there first." She kicked off her boots and set them by the door.

Ruby patted Harbor's hand and asked her to get some mugs for the tea she was making.

"Anything wonderful today?" her mother asked. She wore a simple calico dress with a velvet jacket embroidered in the style of Lapistyr.

Harbor emptied her pockets. When Harbor pulled out the broken necklace chain, her mother said, "Ah, just the thing for your seashell charm."

Harbor placed the toy elephant on the table and gave its head a little shake. She handed her mother the shard of pottery. Her mother held the piece up to the sun and examined it. "How exquisite!"

The sun slanted through the window and across her face. Like Harbor, her cheeks and nose were dotted with freckles. Both had bright green eyes, creamy skin with pink cheeks, and golden-hued hair. Harbor's mother's hair was longer, redder, and fuller, though. Normally she wore it tied back at her neck, but this morning it fell around her face, caught the sun, and made her look like a glowing angel.

"The mugs, dear," Ruby reminded her.

Harbor opened the cabinet, then turned back to her mother. "Mr. Coffin found something interesting, but he wouldn't let me see."

"Mmm," was all her mother said and stirred the eggs in the pan. She reached her hand toward the salt and pepper tins and twisted her wrist. Flakes of white and black danced above the pan, then fell like snow.

Harbor twisted her own wrist, but nothing happened.

"Mugs!" Ruby cried.

Harbor jumped and took down three mugs. Ruby sprinkled herbs into each mug, then, dancing around Coralie, took a steaming kettle from the stove and added the hot water. The two sisters moved around each other easily, the result of growing up together. Harbor wondered what that must be like. She had no siblings. There were no other children on the island at all.

"Your tea, Princess," Ruby said, and handed her a mug. As she did, a puff of pink smoke erupted from it. It smelled of sugar and roses. Ruby clapped her hands together and laughed.

"Ruby!" Harbor cried, but she was laughing as well.

"Just a little birthday treat. Taste it!"

The tea tasted sweet and creamy. Harbor nearly swooned with the deliciousness of it. "It's like fresh cream and berries and honey—"

"Yes, yes," Ruby prompted. "And did you get the mint? A hint of it?"

"Oh, yes," Harbor sighed.

"Perfect!" Ruby said. "I'm so pleased it worked. I've been working on it for days and days. That little puff of smoke is much harder than you'd expect."

"How'd you do it?" Harbor asked.

"She'll never tell her secrets," Harbor's mother said. "The Healers are always the tightest lipped about their magic."

Ruby leaned in close to Harbor. "I'll never share my whole recipe, but that puff of pink was no magic at all. That comes from the deatree leaves—beautiful smoke they make. Whatever color leaf, that's the color of smoke. Pink ones are the hardest to find. I gathered them for ages."

"Well, well," Harbor's mother said as she placed eggs and toast on plates. "I never thought I'd see the day."

"I'm meant to teach her about these things. All the herbs and such." Ruby patted her stomach, quite pleased with herself.

They sat together at the blue table below the window. Her mother returned her attention to the small piece of pottery. "Now, this is something." She turned it over in her hands. "See the little flowers there? Look below."

Harbor took the piece from her mother's warm hand. Its edges were, of course, dull, or Harbor wouldn't be allowed to touch it at all. There, beneath the petals of a flower, a tiny face peeked out.

"It's a cat," her mother explained.

Harbor longed to see a real cat, one outside of the pages of a book.

"Remember that cat I had?" Coralie asked Ruby.

"The little black one? Oh, how you doted on that sweet thing!" Ruby answered.

"It always liked to sit under the thrones. Father hated that!"

They laughed together at this shared memory, and Harbor felt a familiar ache.

"When we go back," Harbor said, speaking slowly. Talk of returning to Lapistyr was often shunned, as though merely speaking of it would keep it from happening. "Do you think I could have a kitten?"

"Oh, most certainly." Her mother picked up the elephant, and its head wobbled back and forth. "Mr. Coffin missed this?"

Ruby raised her eyebrows. "He's not known for missing things."

Harbor's mother spread jam on her toast and said, "Perhaps he's kinder than you think. You could consider it a birthday gift."

Harbor squirmed in her seat. Her mother believed everyone was more than they first appeared. More lovely, more kind, more everything. Harbor was not convinced. "Are there elephants in Lapistyr?" she asked.

"No elephants, but we do have manticora," Ruby said, holding her hands up like claws. "Oh, what a beastly creature! A human face with a mane like a lion and tail with a ball of barbs at the end! It has a lovely voice, though. Like one of Desmond's horns."

"You're making that up!" Harbor cried.

"She's not!" her mother said with a laugh. "Once, one chased Amethyst and me right up a tree!"

Harbor's eyes grew wide. "Are there many beasts like that on Lapistyr?"

"No, dear," she said. "You will be quite safe there. I promise."

The promise felt like warm honeyed sunshine and put Harbor's mind at ease. Her mother was very good at telling tales, and sometimes Harbor wasn't sure if they were all the way true. Her favorite story was the one of how she had met Harbor's father. In Lapistyr, it is the youngest daughter who wears the crown of queen. When she is old enough to take on this role, she goes out into one of the villages disguised as a common girl. There she lives until she falls in love, and the one who wins her heart becomes the next king. When it was Coralie's turn to find her match, she went to a small, seaside village at the northern end of the island. There, on her very first day, she met a sailor fresh from a far northern kingdom. He caught her as she slipped on the pier, nearly falling into the ocean. Their courtship was quick, though she never once revealed her identity until she asked for his hand in marriage. When she did, he revealed his own secret: he, too, was of a royal line, a prince of Benspeir. It was a controversy at the time. The whole point of the exercise was to find a king from among the people, and Coralie had gone and found a foreign prince. When they married, her father's brothers had made him give up all his claims to Benspeir and then fallen into fighting about who should have his claim. But when Coralie told the story, she giggled and her whole face glowed, and Harbor knew her parents were truly forever and always in love.

"Hurry now," Ruby said to Harbor. "We can't be reminiscing all morning. I've met you here for our lesson because we've got some gathering to do and I want to go into town this morning. Change your clothes and comb your hair, and we'll be on our way."

Though Ruby had told her to hurry, Harbor wanted to put her shell on the necklace chain she had found. It was tangled, and she carefully unknotted it as she spoke to Sweetwater and Lucretia, her dolls who sat on her bed with their eyes staring straight out in front of them. Sweetwater was made of porcelain. When she'd arrived, her face was blank, so Opal Pearl had painted a new one on for her, with eyes of green and freckles across her cheeks, like Harbor. Lucretia was made of something Mr. Coffin had called plastic. She was not much bigger than Harbor's hand, her body molded and stiff, with arms and legs that moved on a pivot. She had a big *L* printed on the center of her chest.

"Mum told me about manticora today. What a strange creature. I wonder if everything will seem strange to me when I go back?"

Harbor had been thinking more and more about returning to Lapistyr. She only needed to make it safely through one more year, and then she would be free from the danger of her curse and they could all return home. She was sure it was the most beautiful land in all the world. Plus, her father was there, so her family could all be together again.

She had also gotten it into her head this was the year her magic would develop. Her mother and her aunts each had magic, as had all the women in the Lapistyr royal family, but it had shown up at different ages for each of them. Her mother's, weak as it was, hadn't revealed itself until she was fourteen. Still, Harbor was certain this was her year—any day now, really—and no one could convince her otherwise.

She held the necklace chain, now untangled, to show her dolls. "Got it!" she said. She found the shell she had saved and laced it onto the chain and then put it around her neck. "How do I look, girls? Have to look fancy for my big birthday."

The hem of her dress had gotten wet, and so she changed into a blouse and a pinafore with short pants under the skirt. Ada Flynn had made the pinafore for Harbor and, knowing her proclivity for collecting, had put six pockets into it.

She gave a wave to her dolls and went downstairs to meet her aunt.

CHAPTER FOUR

Ruby's job was to teach Harbor about the trees. Benspeir, the homeland of Harbor's father, drew its strength and wealth from the trees that grew tall and strong on their land. There was hope that someday the Kingdom of Benspeir would stop its infighting and their alliance could be remade. It was important for Harbor to know all about the trees that grew in her father's homeland, as well as those on Small Island and in Lapistyr. Ruby, though, sometimes strayed. "I am to teach you of the trees and things that grow," Ruby had once said. "And if along the way I teach how to use the leaves of one or another to make a salve for a scrape or a broken heart—well, that shouldn't be a bother to anyone, should it?"

Ruby readjusted her satchel over her shoulder. She wore it whenever she was out of the house. It was full of tinctures and bandages and whatnot so she might help any person or creature who needed it.

Outside, Harbor and Ruby found Opal Pearl perched on the very top of a tall ladder, one foot extended out behind her as she leaned forward with an orange stone in her hand. She reached toward a crook in a tree where, already, she had placed three other stones. The ladder shook and Opal Pearl with it. Harbor froze in the doorway.

"Since you have arrived at precisely the right time," Opal Pearl said with hardly a quaver in her voice, "perhaps you might steady the ladder?"

Harbor did as she was told, bracing the ladder with her hands while Ruby bustled below, wringing her hands together. "How many times have I told you, Opal Pearl, we are too old for ladder climbing! Have Frank place your trinkets."

Opal Pearl scrambled down the ladder and threw one of her long braids over her shoulder. "If you are afraid to climb ladders, that is a question of your character, not age. I am perfectly fine climbing them. It's just that my arms aren't quite as long as they need to be. Further, I cannot have Frank placing my objects. He has no magic in him. Finally, I would be much obliged if you refrained from calling my artwork 'trinkets.'"

Though her argument was long and well constructed, she said it all with a smile and Ruby responded with a laugh.

Opal Pearl, the second eldest of Harbor's aunts, was a Protector by her magic and an artist by passion.

"Why didn't you just fling it up there?" Harbor asked.

"Fling it? You want me to just fling my art?" She laughed. "Why, that's worse than calling it a trinket!"

"No, I mean magic it," Harbor tried to explain. "Wiggle your fingers and send it up there."

"Wiggle your fingers!" Ruby exclaimed with a terrific guffaw.

"I find meaning and form in the act of placing the objects," Opal Pearl said. "Understand?" She chucked Harbor under the chin with a crooked finger. Opal Pearl's hands were gnarled like the limbs of the plumrose tree. If she had a birthday, Harbor didn't know when it was or how many she'd had, but she was old. Her hair was white, except for the ends that were blackish gray. Her white skin was wrinkled, deep crevasses around her eyes and mouth. Her eyes were a milky blue. Her fingers were nimble, though.

Harbor smiled at her. "Does that have something to do with my birthday?" she asked.

Opal Pearl's smile faltered. "Not precisely." She tucked her hands into the pockets of her overalls. "Rocks are steadying, you know. It's always a good idea to steady our island, wouldn't you say?"

Harbor agreed, though it was unclear to her how putting rocks in trees helped their island.

"Do you need any more help?" Ruby asked.

"No," Opal Pearl said. "Best be on your way."

Ruby handed Harbor a basket, and the two began their way down the curving road. When they were out of earshot of Opal Pearl, Harbor asked, "What are we hunting for today? Mugwort? Lamb's cress?"

"Rose hips," Ruby said. "It's jamming time."

While Harbor did love the jam Ruby made from the bright rose hips that grew on the beach rose bushes all over the island, she had been hoping for something a little more magical, especially on her birthday. "I thought perhaps you could teach me something else. Something more . . . *advanced*. I am twelve today, you know."

"Oh, I know, dear," Ruby said as she opened the door. "I think the whole world knows it."

"The whole world?"

"The whole world and The Somewhere Else as well." Ruby was one of the few people who even mentioned The Somewhere Else to Harbor, that strange land out of sight and out of range. As they walked, Ruby made the blooms on the flowers open beside them, and the fragrances danced around them.

"Like that!" Harbor said. "How do you do that? Can you teach me?"

Ruby frowned at the flowers. They closed right back up, tucking their secrets and their smells away with them. "Is that what you're going on about, Harbor dear? Magic? You know I cannot be teaching you about magic. Only Opal Pearl and Sapphire can do that."

Harbor gave her aunt a pleading look.

Ruby sighed. "This is what I can tell you: there's all kinds of magic. Every bit of nature has some magic, I would say. Some of us are just better at seeing it. Those flowers love to bloom and share their fragrance. I've just got to coax them with a bit of Small Magic. That's what I use, Harbor. Small Magic. Just enough to make the tinctures and teas work."

Though Ruby had not told her much, it was more than anyone had told her in all her years. "If there is Small Magic, does that mean there is also Big Magic?"

Ruby shook her head. "Sapphire. Sapphire has the sight, and so she determines when we may do Big Magic, and it's she who will tell you about it."

Harbor did not like this answer, but she wouldn't allow it to dissuade her. "What about me? I must have some Small Magic. What is it?"

Ruby nearly dropped her basket on the ground. "Oh, Harbor, I'm not certain I can say. Anyway, you're too young for your magic to show up yet."

Harbor's heart beat faster. "I'm not! Sapphire's came when she was eleven."

"And your mother's when she was fourteen. There's no telling when or if or how it will come."

"But I'm certain it will be this year. Before we go back. It has to!" Then she paused. "What do you mean 'if'?"

"If? I'm sure I didn't mean anything by it." She tugged on the strap of her satchel.

"I will have magic, right?"

"Yes," Ruby said. But she couldn't look at Harbor. "Maybe. It's all very . . . complicated." She put the basket down and then placed her warm hands on Harbor's cheeks. "Please don't ask me any more about it, dear. I'll surely say the wrong thing."

Harbor's body slumped, but she felt bad for Ruby and decided not to ask any more questions. They continued down the path, gathering rose hips as they went. Hod Templeton nodded a hello as he walked up the hill to his pasture where he kept two milking cows and a dozen sheep. "Good morning, Mr. Templeton," Ruby said to him.

"Morning, ma'am. Morning, Harbor."

"How are you today?" she asked.

"Fair to middlin'," he replied. This was always how Hod replied to the question of how he was doing.

"Wonderful to hear," Ruby said. "May you have all the blessings of this fine day."

"Ayuh, you as well," he replied and was on his way.

They stopped to pick at another patch of rose hips when Harbor noticed something a little deeper in. A purple flower, shaped almost like a tiny hat. She reached her hand in and plucked the bloom. "Look," she said to Ruby.

Ruby's eyes went wide. "Drop that at once!"

Harbor did as she was told. The flower fell to the ground. "What? What is it? There are no thorns. I checked."

At that moment, Opal Pearl and Harbor's mother came around the bend, arm in arm.

"Is everything okay?" Coralie asked.

Ruby shook her head. "That's gullsbane, my dear. Deadly roots on that plant. Where'd you find it?"

Harbor stepped back as she pointed to the bush. "In there. It's growing in among the roses."

"Strange," Ruby said as she peered in. "The flower will do you no harm, nor the stem. The roots have the power. They can kill you dead if you ingest enough. A drop of it can set someone right to sleep." She reached in and touched the plant. "I didn't know we had any on the island. Best not eat any of the rose hips that share a root bed with those." She took Harbor's basket and dumped out the whole lot.

"Ruby!" Harbor cried, looking at her morning's work thrown on the path.

"We can't eat them now. The roots talk to each other. They share things. Some good, some bad."

Harbor wasn't sure about this. Plants could not actually talk to one another, or share things, but she supposed it was possible the poison of the gullsbane root could seep into the rose hips.

Harbor's mother gave Harbor's shoulders a gentle squeeze. "It's lucky you were with Ruby when you found that."

Ruby snapped her fingers, and the rose hips withered at once, browning and crumpling in on themselves. They crumbled to dust. With a flick of her wrist, Ruby set the dust flying.

"Wait! Didn't you just let the poison into the air?" Harbor asked.

"I broke it down into the tiniest bits that couldn't hurt a soul. It's when it's concentrated that it's a problem. If those rose hips were poisoned and a bird grabbed one, the poor creature would surely die. Sometimes you have to let things go to make them lose their power." In the sky, the dust had nearly disappeared.

"Have you ever seen that flower on this island before?" Opal Pearl asked.

Ruby admitted she had not. The three sisters exchanged a look.

"I'm sure it's nothing," Ruby said. "It's a plant that likes to move. It might have been in the forest all this time, and this is just one little shoot—"

"I don't like there being things on this island we don't know about," Opal Pearl said.

"We should make sure to eradicate it all. At once," Coralie said decisively. Harbor could always tell when her mother took on the role of queen. She stood taller. Her voice rang deeper.

Ruby hesitated, but then said, "Indeed. I'll start on that now."

"You should go on down to the hotel," Coralie told her. "I'm sure Brigid won't mind if you're early for your lesson."

"Very well," Harbor said, though she didn't want to leave her mother and aunts. As she turned to go, she noticed Ruby wrapping some of the gullsbane roots in a small scrap of leather and tucking them into her satchel. What in the good graces was she doing? Harbor had never known Ruby to defy the queen.

Her mother prodded her along, so Harbor went down the path. Since she had plenty of time, she strayed to the rocks where she looked for snails and crabs. She found a hermit crab with a shell of gold and claws of purple. "Good morning, fellow princess," she said to the hermit crab. As there were no other children on the island, she often found herself talking to the animals. "Do you have magical aunts? Do they keep secrets from one another?"

Before the hermit crab could answer, or skitter away, the nine o'clock chimes sounded. "Oh no! I'm meant to be with Brigid now!" Harbor took off at a run, hoping she might sneak to the stables at the back of the Murphy Hotel without Leo Murphy seeing her. Even though she did not have any lessons scheduled with Leo that day, he still paid careful attention to her comings and goings and always gave her an earful if she was late. Perhaps he might spare her a little kindness and forgive her tardiness, especially on her birthday. Knowing Leo, it wasn't likely. Giving an earful was his favorite thing to do, and she was sure she was in for it.

CHAPTER FIVE

Harbor sprinted toward the center of the village and the grand old hotel that stood proudly there. Elaborate columns carved of wood held up an overhang that created a shaded porch.

Harbor was a fast runner, but not fast enough.

Leo Murphy stood on the steps of the hotel holding his pocket watch as Harbor ran up the path. When she stood in front of him, he snapped the watch shut and dropped it into the pocket of his blazer made of deep green worsted wool and trimmed in satin. The pocket swallowed the watch, leaving only the gold, glinting chain visible.

"You are one minute and forty-seven seconds late for your exercises with Brigid."

"I was picking rose hips with Ruby and well—you see—"

"What do I see?" Leo demanded.

"We lost track of time."

Archie, who sat in one of the rockers on the porch polishing his boots of golden leather, grinned. "Is it jamming season already?"

Leo frowned. "Time is not something one should lose track of. It's a very careless thing to do. Further, jam is not part of the curriculum of a princess."

"Perhaps it should be," Harbor said.

"I concur," Archie said. "There simply isn't a greater pleasure than fresh jam. Jam on warm toast, that's a meal fit for kings and queens."

Leo's frown deepened. "Elocution, classics, music, art, horsemanship, physical education, and court manners. These are the subjects a princess must learn."

"I think a princess should know of many things," Harbor replied. "Especially practical things."

"Hear, hear," Archie agreed.

Leo gave him a withering look. "This is why, Archibald, you were not invited to be one of Harbor's teachers."

Archie winked at Harbor, his thick white eyebrow wiggling like a snowy caterpillar.

Leo cleared his throat. "Punctuality is the height of etiquette. While it is true that the queen is never late, a princess can be. She should endeavor not to be so."

Leo oversaw Harbor's instruction in courtly manners. They met once a week and practiced things like walking while she held his arm or eating soup without slurping. Though it was not one of their days for lessons, he would never miss an opportunity to lecture her on princess propriety.

Harbor bent deeply at the waist. "I apologize, Master Murphy, for my tardiness. I would say it will never happen again, but I think we both know that is not the case."

This made Archie laugh and earned a scowl from Leo, though it must be said that nearly everything made Leo scowl.

Standing straight again and looking Leo right in the eye as she had been taught, she said, "A little bird told me you were organizing my party."

Leo scowled even more deeply. "What makes you think a child as poorly behaved as you will be having a party?"

Archie said, "I remember turning twelve. Those were the days. Roaming free among the rocks and caves. Why once I saw a—"

Leo cut him off. "Brigid is waiting for you," he said to Harbor.

"Yes, Leo," Harbor said. Remembering herself, she added, "May you have all the blessings of this fine day."

"May you as well," he replied.

Harbor hurried into the hotel. Inside, the lobby floor was made of black-and-white marble in a checkerboard pattern. Shoes clicked across it and sounded very official, which was why Harbor liked to go barefoot.

Hanging in the lobby was an old iron chandelier with tiny light bulbs that cast only the smallest bit of light. The front desk stood to the right of the lobby, though no one ever checked in or out. Tommy Murphy sat behind the desk with a squat hat on top of his head. "Good morning, Harbor!"

"Morning!" she replied, not even bothering to slow down. Tommy didn't worry so much about manners. He was quite pleased to sit at the front desk, read his books, and gather gossip.

She ran across the black-and-white tiles and threw open the door to the ballroom. Archie kept the parquet floor gleaming and beat the velvet curtains once a week to keep the dust off them. Light spilled in through the floor-to-ceiling windows.

In the center of the ballroom, under a chandelier of cascading crystal, stood Brigid Murphy with her hands on her hips.

"I'm sorry!" Harbor cried. "Leo stopped me!"

Without a word, Brigid lunged at Harbor, fencing foil drawn. She swung. The foil *whizzed* as it sliced the air.

Without thinking, Harbor jumped. She tucked her knees to her chest. The foil cut beneath her feet.

Brigid slipped her foil back into its scabbard. "Nicely done."

"You nearly whipped me!" Harbor exclaimed.

"A fencer must always be at the ready."

Brigid was not yet twenty, with a puff of auburn hair, warm brown skin, and her own dusting of freckles. She had an unconventional style of teaching; that was what everyone said. Still, Harbor was coming along quite nicely as a fencer.

Everyone on the island said that, too: she was quick, sure of hand, and clever with her moves. Her archery was another question altogether.

"Let's begin," Brigid said.

The two parried back and forth, each landing glancing strikes. Brigid called out the score as they went along. In the end, Harbor was the winner. She wasn't sure if Brigid had let her win to boost her confidence or because she was simply tired of the game. Together, they went outside to drink cool water from the fountain.

"It's not at all like a real battle," Brigid said, wiping water from her chin.

The cool water coursed down Harbor's throat. "What's a real battle like?"

The two of them lay side by side and stared at the blue sky.

"There's no keeping score, for starters," Brigid said. "A glancing blow doesn't gain you any points. You need to take your foe out of the battle completely."

"Completely?"

"The swords clash together hard enough to shake your arms. Sometimes they spark. And the heat! They call it the heat of battle—you're sweating and your muscles are burning." She propped herself on her elbows. "But some of it's like a dance, too. Like your body has been taken over and you are moving to some unknown choreography. They're coming at you, again and again. They don't want to lose either. Sometimes they are so close you can—"

"Brigid Murphy!" Leo Murphy cried. "Such talk is not appropriate for a young princess to hear."

"Oughten she to know what struggles her soldiers will face?" Brigid asked.

"She has no soldiers. She is on this peaceful island. There's no need for you to fill her head with senseless tales."

"Senseless tales?" Brigid sat up again, streaks of pink on her cheeks.

Leo smirked. "I suggest you keep to true stories."

Harbor looked from Brigid to Leo, confused.

"She tells a good yarn," Leo said. "But she's never been in battle. She's but a girl herself."

Brigid scowled but said nothing. Harbor supposed it was true. Brigid had come to the island only a few years before, when she was just seventeen, too young to be a soldier. Being on the island, she'd never had her chance.

When Leo left them be, Brigid said, "Don't worry. A princess will never have to fight in a real battle."

"Are you sure?" Harbor asked.

"Of course. Never has a princess or queen of Lapistyr gone to battle." She hesitated. "Then again, Lapistyr never had a military before King Ash arrived."

Harbor rolled onto her side. "Really?"

"Oh, yes," Brigid said. "He brought a crew of soldiers with him. You know I am among the first from Lapistyr to join the military. All the other soldiers were from Benspeir. I aim to do our people proud should that war ever come."

Harbor was reminded again of her curse. It was nearly impossible to go a day—an hour even—without thinking about it.

"But I'm twelve today," Harbor said. "I only need to make it one more year, and then the curse will be over. The war won't come."

"Perhaps," Brigid said.

"If it does come, I will be able to use my magic to keep you safe. If I'm a Protector, then I shall wrap you all in an impenetrable shield. And if I am a Healer, I will send you off to battle with wagons full of cures."

"If you are a Seer, you could tell us the enemy's plans," Brigid said. "That would be most useful."

"If I'm a Shifter, I could help you with disguises!"

"I could be a spy!" Brigid said excitedly.

The only magic they hadn't touched on was that of her mother, the queen. A Feeler. She could sense the emotions of others. It did not seem a very useful magic, and Harbor hoped that would not be the one she got. Each of them could also do the Small Magic Ruby had told her about—little tricks like sprinkling salt on the eggs without touching the shaker—but, as the youngest, the queen was weak in that, too.

"So," Brigid said. "If the war does come, you will surely be able to protect us all. For now, though, let's enjoy this fine day and go for a ride." She adopted Leo's tone: "A princess must be a fine equestrian, after all."

They rode the ponies around the island. Harbor rode sidesaddle through the village, but as soon as they crested the hill, she switched her seat and the two rode the ponies as fast as the small animals would go through the green fields of blueberries and to the cliffs on the far side of the island that fell to the churning water below. They squinted and wished they could see Lapistyr in the distance.

Brigid, Harbor knew, missed Lapistyr terribly. She missed her twin brother and her lady love. She missed the pomp of the royal guard. She missed, most of all, her chance to be a true soldier. She told Harbor stories of the island, which was more than anyone else would do. Oh, they told her the tales, honorable and proud, but not the day-to-day details Harbor so longed to hear. Only Brigid told her how the merchants would squawk at one another in the market or how each day the royal groundskeepers spread new pebbles in front of the castle.

"I suppose they are having the same weather as we. It's almost time for the high-summer festival. Oh, you would love it!" Brigid listed all the foods they would eat: oysters, clams, and mussels, strawberry rhubarb pies, fish longer than a person stuffed with sweet pork and peaches from the orchard.

"Next year," Harbor said. "I will see it with my own eyes."

"That you will. And you will ride on a proper horse." Brigid gave a deep sigh.

They rode back to the stables by the Murphy Hotel,

passing through their little town that each knew as well as they knew their own hearts. Harbor waved to people as she rode by—Hod Templeton by the general store, Ada Flynn out on his porch—but Brigid rode with her head down, lost in thought.

Soon, Harbor thought. *Soon this will be over, and we can all go home.*

CHAPTER SIX

*H*ome was a strange word for Harbor. The leaning cottage she shared with her mother, the Murphy Hotel, the village, and Small Island itself all held the warmth and familiarity that Harbor expected she should feel for her home. Yet it felt as though everything on Small Island was temporary. She knew her true home was on Lapistyr—a distant island she didn't know at all.

She thought of home and voyages and magic as she walked through town. The smell of the ocean whipped its way to her. She didn't know any other smell but that salty air. The salt was part of her blood. All this time she'd been thinking of *returning* to Lapistyr, she hadn't given much thought to *leaving* Small Island behind. It gave her a funny, not-at-all-pleasant feeling.

She made her way down the main lane and went up the old, marble steps of the library. It was a large, brick building, nearly as large as the hotel, with an imposing wooden door. Harbor pulled the door open and stepped into the hush.

Mr. Broom turned the pages of an old book at one of the study tables. Some of the other regulars were there, too, seated in their usual spots. Perched cross-legged on top of the circulation desk was Amethyst, Harbor's youngest aunt. She jumped down when Harbor entered. "Harbor!" she cried out, as though Harbor didn't come every day as part of her lessons.

"I have questions," Harbor told her.

"I have books!" Amethyst spread her arms wide. "What are your questions?"

"Are manticora real and are elephants? Do all women in the royal line of Lapistyr get magic? Why did my father bring an army to Lapistyr?"

"My, what a lot of questions spinning around in your head this morning! Let's see." She tapped her lips, then hurried to a wooden cabinet of small drawers. She pulled one out and began rifling through the small cards tucked inside. "Ah! Found it. Wait here!" She ran into the stacks and came back with two bestiaries, one from Lapistyr and one from The Somewhere Else.

"Those should answer your first questions. As for the others, those are bigger questions. Shall we tackle magic first or the army?"

Harbor wanted to know both things, but the magic was the deeper mystery. Whatever reason her father had for bringing an army with him to Lapistyr, she was sure it was a good one. "Magic," she said.

Amethyst spun around. "Come with me."

Harbor's heartbeat quickened as she followed Amethyst to the back of the library, her arms loaded down with the books. She worried she had asked the wrong kind of question, the kind that might bring them into The Locked Room, which held, according to Amethyst, boring old things like ledgers and books about statistics. Harbor had only been into it once, with Amethyst, to retrieve a book on rubber-soled shoes for Mr. Coffin after a box full of rain boots had washed up. When Harbor had asked why the boring books were the ones locked up, Amethyst said they were being punished for their tediousness.

Thankfully, they skipped The Locked Room and Amethyst led her up two flights of stairs to the small quarters where Amethyst lived. "Sorry for the mess," Amethyst said, but Harbor didn't mind at all. Harbor had always loved Amethyst's rooms. They were filled with books, of course, but also trinkets and decorations that sparkled. Clothes were tossed about in piles and draped over furniture, colors and textures swirling together.

Amethyst found an old silk robe with orange orchids printed on it. As she slipped it on, the orchids changed to pale pink roses. She dug through a pile of clothes until she found another robe, this one golden yellow and embroidered with tiny blueberries. She held it in her hands and closed her eyes. The yellow faded and swirls of green seeped in. "Here you go," she said, handing the robe to Harbor. "We ought to be properly fancy for such an important conversation."

Harbor put the robe on, the silk cool against her skin.

From her vanity, Amethyst picked up a small mirror with an intricately carved ivory handle. She held it up to Harbor. "What do you see?"

Harbor saw only herself.

"Look closer," Amethyst prompted.

"I'm trying," Harbor said. She squinted at the mirror.

"Just tell me what you see."

Harbor saw herself, searching and longing, staring back at her. "All I see is me!"

"Precisely! Each of us, our very existence is magical—though, of course, you are especially magical to me. Each person, each tree, each stone—especially the stones—"

"Amethyst!" Harbor cried, feeling sour that she had been tricked. "That's not what I meant."

"I'm not being cute here, Harbor. There *is* power and energy in everything around us. Think of magic like gathering power and then releasing it—with a purpose." She led Harbor to the window where they looked out at the sea. "Like waves. The water is gathered and then crashes against the rocks."

"That's not magic," Harbor said. "That's the moon and the tides."

"What I mean to say is, some people are able to gather that power and then redirect it."

Harbor thought of what Ruby had said about coaxing the flowers to bloom. It had to be more than that, though.

"Perhaps it's easiest to explain with Ruby. She gathers herbs and plants and mixes them together. Each of those herbs and plants has a power, and she combines them. Take the humble coneflower, for example. What does Ruby get from that?"

"Echinacea. It helps to keep you healthy."

"Right, and you or I or anyone else might make a tea of it and stave off a cold. Ruby taps into something deeper. The energy of the whole plant, from its roots to its flowers. She quite literally gathers the energy in the plants and then uses her magic to redirect it. Why, under Ruby's care, something as simple as echinacea could stop the worst of plagues in its tracks."

"This morning she made a tea for me with deatree leaves, and it sent up a puff of pink smoke."

"Precisely! Any one of us could burn those leaves for color, but Ruby used her magic to put them into the tea to make a little surprise for you."

"She also—" Harbor hesitated, but told Amethyst about the gullsbane and the roots she had seen Ruby hide away.

Amethyst thought on it for a moment, then said, "I am certain she did it for a very good reason. Ruby can't stand to see a living thing destroyed, even a dangerous one." Amethyst moved from the window, the sun behind her. "But let's get back to our magic talk. Consider Opal Pearl. In any society, she would be an artist. A good one. Her work would have power over people—to make them think or feel, to awe them. But she's able to gather energy into her art and use that to protect us."

"Is that Small Magic or Big Magic?" Harbor asked.

"Someone's been talking to you," Amethyst teased. She ran her hand through her curls. "It's not truly Big Magic, but I'm not sure I would call what Opal Pearl does small. Her magic is very strong. Nearly as strong as Sapphire's. Sometimes I think it's because she worked so hard at it. Sometimes I think that's just how it is. Some of us get lots of it while others get less, like some people can run very fast or shoot very straight. Practice helps, but there's something else."

"What about you?" Harbor asked. "How do you do the color thing?"

"Oh, I don't know," Amethyst said. "I see colors all around me. In music and in words and in stories and in things. I concentrate and hold the item, and it becomes the color it ought to be in that moment." She gave a little shrug, and her bracelets jingled together. "Sapphire thinks it's frivolous. Unfocused. Maybe it is."

"I think it's wonderful," Harbor said. "I often hope I will be a Shifter like you."

"And that's why you are my favorite child in all the world." Amethyst hugged Harbor close. "My power lies in beauty, which not everyone values," she said, then tapped her lips and turned them a deep shade of red. "I think beauty is what makes life worth living."

"But how did you end up in the library? What's that got to do with beauty?"

Amethyst's perfectly plucked eyebrows shot up. "Harbor Rose! Is there anything more beautiful than words strung together to make a poem or a story? I would roll around in those words and cover myself from head to toe if I could."

"You could," Harbor said.

"I suppose you're right!" Amethyst tapped her robe. Words danced over it, falling into lines of poetry. "Glorious!" She swayed from side to side and made the words dance. Then, all at once, she remembered herself. "You know I'm not meant to talk about all this with you."

"I know. It's just that—"

"Just that you feel you ought to know when it's something that relates to you. I was the same way, always wanting to know when our magic would come and what it would be. And there was Sapphire and Opal Pearl telling us to be patient, which was just maddening. There's nothing that makes someone less patient than telling them to be patient."

"Exactly!" Harbor said. There was relief in knowing someone knew how she felt.

"Sometimes people fear that knowledge will harm you. I think it can only protect us."

"But how can it harm me to know if I will get my magic? I know you can't tell me when, but Ruby said *if* and I don't like that word *if*!"

"It's a truly terrible word," Amethyst agreed. "The problem is you are asking about magic as if it's a straightforward thing we can know about and study and write down in a book. It's never so simple as that, and when it comes to your special case—"

"My special case?" Harbor asked and immediately regretted interrupting.

Amethyst blinked. "I would tell you more, Harbor, I would, but I must go by what my sisters agreed to. When the time is right, we will tell you your whole story. I promise." Amethyst smiled. "Now, if your mother or anyone else asks what we learned today, tell them all about manticora and elephants, okay?"

"Okay," Harbor said with a laugh. They flopped onto Amethyst's bed, and each chose a book. Harbor read about manticora and other beasts, and Amethyst read a love story. That strange feeling poked again at Harbor: the sense she was losing something, like the tide pulling back. She glanced at Amethyst, at her kind eyes and easy smile, and pushed the thought away.

∂∂∂∂

When Harbor and Amethyst went back downstairs into the library, Mr. Broom was still at his table, still staring at a single page. "Sweet Harbor!" he called to her. "What a gem you are. Ever since you were a babe with Mr. Coffin down by the sea, I knew you were a treasure. I saw an elephant once, you know."

"Really?" Harbor asked.

"There was a circus ship out on the ocean. What year was that? Never mind. A circus ship! The *Royal Tar*, she was called. Had a whole caravan of animals. Tiger, horses, camels, snakes, and that elephant. She was headed out of Eastport, up the coast."

"Where's—" Harbor began, but Mr. Broom was in his storytelling mode, and he kept going.

"They took some of the lifeboats off to make room for all the animals. All that weight and poor weather, it caught fire, it did. The people jumped off the ship, but the animals were in their cages."

"Oh no!" Harbor said.

"Oh yes!" Mr. Broom replied. "Now some folks say those animals all went down with the ship. Others say the tiger made it ashore, and the snakes, too. Say you can still find them on Deer Isle."

It was another place Harbor had never heard of, but that wasn't too unusual. Mr. Broom was very, very old, and he peppered his stories with people and places that probably never existed.

"But I tell you I saw, with my own very eyes, that elephant swimming. It was years after the crash. My pa and I were out in our fishing boat, and we see this gray mass. First, we think it's a rock, though there's never been a rock there before. Next, we think it's a whale. But then that elephant stuck its trunk out of the water. Sprayed the ocean on us like it was a firehose." Mr. Broom laughed.

"Then what?" Harbor gasped.

"We took the boat home. Already had our catch for the day."

"No, Mr. Broom! To the elephant?"

"Why it kept on swimming. I called for it to follow us back to Dirigo, but it had its own plan."

"That is quite a story, Mr. Broom," Amethyst said to him. She took Harbor's hand and led her to the library door. "You know he's a little mixed up," Amethyst said. "Those places he mentions—"

"And the circus animals—"

"Right," Amethyst said. "It's his dreams and the books he's read and the stories he's heard. All a jumble. He's a very old man. Very kind and very wise, but very old." She kissed Harbor on the top of her head. "Hurry along now. I'll see you tonight!"

CHAPTER SEVEN

Frank Swan sat on the steps of the general store whittling a piece of wood. He was not yet thirty, with thick, dark curls that he often wore under a knit cap.

"There she is," he said as she reached him. "All twelve years of her. How's her Royal Highness today?"

"Did you know Mr. Broom once saw an elephant?" she replied. "Or so he said."

"Mr. Broom says a lot of things. When I was a boy, he was the one who told me all about the giants. Swore they were real." A grin broke through his worried expression. "Just wait until I'm old and doddering. I'll tell the best stories. Like the one about the princess who grew up right here on Small Island. She used to help me fish!"

Now it was Harbor's turn to frown. "But when I go back, won't you go back with me?"

"This is my home, Harbor," he told her. "I couldn't possibly live anywhere else. Why, I think I might be stuck here as tight as a barnacle to a rock."

She and Frank fished together each day, and Frank taught her about the sea, which no one had bothered to teach her about, even though it surrounded them. She wasn't sure what she would do without him.

Flakes of sawdust fell as he worked the wood, his hands and the knife moving quickly. He stopped and held the wood out to her. It was a little girl.

"Why, it's me!" she exclaimed. She recognized herself in the way the girl's hair fell and her uneven hem.

"It will be," he said. "I've got to paint it up for you. But you can add it to your collection soon enough."

"Where'd you learn to do that?" she asked.

"My father taught me," he said. "And his father before."

Harbor hadn't known that Frank *had* a father. Frank lived all alone and had no family to speak of. "Did he die?" she asked.

Frank's gaze flicked out to the lighthouse, then back at her. "He left. A long time ago. My mother, too. They wanted a different life than what they could find on Small Island."

"And you didn't go with them?"

"Like I said. I'm a barnacle. Now, are we going to yap all day or get some fishing done?"

He slipped the knife and wooden girl into his pockets and rose to his full height. He wasn't a tall man, a full six inches shorter than her father, she estimated, but there was a bigness to him. A warmth.

51

Inside the general store, there were bins of fresh vegetables and shelves of canned ones. Smoked fish was right by the register, and there was a cooler with the fish Frank and others caught and chickens that Hod Templeton butchered himself. There was milk and butter from Hod's cows. Best of all were the pies and buckles and other treats that Hod's wife, Mary, made. Harbor's favorite was the strawberry rhubarb crisp baked at the start of summertime.

Hod was behind the counter, which was strange. Usually Mary was there, but Hod told them she was in the back, baking up a special order.

"What kind of special order?" Harbor asked.

"Never you mind," Hod said, then winked at her, and Harbor knew Mary was working on something special for her for her birthday.

Harbor wandered around the store looking at the neat rows of cans and wishing there was still some of the berry jewel candy that had been in the last shipment from Lapistyr.

"Chuppta?" Hod asked Frank.

"Fishin'," Frank said, and laughed because Frank hardly ever got up to anything else.

"Winds been whipping. Best to watch out in case a storm blows in."

"Aye, I've got my eyeballs on it. And this one's got a knack for tellin' when something's brewing."

Frank had taught Harbor how to look out to the horizon

to check the weather. You could see the streaks of rain against the sky, sometimes when it was still miles away.

"Real girl of the island, that one," Hod said.

"This'll do," Frank said. With bait in hand, he and Harbor made their way to the dock. When they got to their fishing spot, he handed her rod to her, the bait already on the hook. She wasn't allowed to touch the hooks, on account of the danger of being pricked.

From their spot, they could see Ruby wading into the water. A seal popped its head up, and Ruby held out her hand. The seal swam closer and ate right from Ruby's palm.

"Days used to be a seal would know to stay far away from a person."

"Ruby's not a regular person," Harbor said. "She's a Healer. I wonder if that seal is hurt."

"Mights be," Frank replied.

They fished in silence, squinting against the sun that warmed their cheeks. In general, Healer wasn't near the top of her list for the type of magic she hoped to get, but when she saw Ruby tending to seals and such, it seemed like it might be a nice one to have after all.

"When I go back to Lapistyr, I suppose I won't fish anymore."

"Why's that?" Frank asked.

"A princess doesn't normally catch her own food," Harbor said glumly. "I don't think a queen ever does. I've had all these lessons about literature and art and music, but that's only a small part of being a queen. Perhaps I'm not ready at all? I think I ought to be prepared for all eventualities."

"So you're wanting queen lessons from me now?" Frank asked with a laugh.

Just then, there was a tug on his line. A smile flashed on his lips before he set to reeling it in. Carefully he pulled in the line, let the fish tug, then pulled some more until the fish was thrashing at the surface of the water. He gave one final pull, and the fish arched through the air and landed, as if thrown, in Frank's hand. Instead of throwing it in their basket, he tossed it down. The fish lay, shiny and still, on the dock. "Princess Harbor, I have my first queening lesson for you. This fish has been caught. How do you distribute it?"

"You caught it, Frank. It's your fish."

"Is that your command?" he asked.

"It's what's fair."

"Ah, but what about Mary Templeton? She's too busy baking to catch any fish."

"You could trade with her."

"Or old Mr. Broom. He can't fish at all."

"You could share it with him," Harbor said. "He'd like that very much, I'm sure. And he'd be good company for you for dinner."

"But it's not my fish," Frank said. "It came out of your royal ocean. You're the one who needs to decide. Maybe you ought to give it to you and your aunts. You are the royal family, after all. Or perhaps you should have it smoked and give a tiny portion to each house."

Harbor thought on it. She frowned. "I'm not sure. There are too many choices."

"That's why I'm happy to be a plain old fisherman and not a king." Frank tousled her hair. "For now, be a child, Harbor. Enjoy it. Your time to be queen will come soon enough."

Harbor wasn't sure. But it was a beautiful afternoon, and she was with Frank, and so she decided to do as he said and just enjoy it. The storm clouds that were forming were too far off for her to see.

CHAPTER EIGHT

Harbor's mother told her she must be at the party before the clock struck six o'clock, but Harbor was quite caught up sharing her day with Sweetwater and Lucretia. She moved Lucretia's arms and legs so the doll stood on the bed looking proud. "I learned so much about magic today but feel I'm left with less knowledge than when I started. How is that possible?"

As she mused, the clock tower in the village began to chime. "Oh no!" She changed into a fancy dress brought from Lapistyr, ran a comb through her hair, and jammed her feet into the only dressy shoes she owned. As she ran toward the hotel, one shoe fell off, so she kicked them both off and carried them in her hand.

When Amethyst saw Harbor, she gave her a quick once-over and then placed her hands on Harbor's shoulders. With a sharp nod, she turned Harbor's dress, once pale yellow, to a blue that matched the sea. "Much better," Amethyst said. "Yellow washes you out completely." The dress sparkled like a starry night, and Harbor couldn't help but twirl around in it.

Ada Flynn, who happened to be walking by at the time, said, "A regular fairy godmother, you are. Next you'll be turning a pumpkin into a coach."

This made Harbor and Amethyst giggle, and Amethyst said, "With mice for coachmen."

"Mice?" Leo declared from the front porch of the hotel. "There are no mice in this establishment! I assure you of that."

This only made Harbor and Amethyst laugh more. Amethyst offered her arm, and Harbor took it just as Leo had instructed her. The steps of the hotel were lit by glass jars full of glowing berries. Ruby had picked the berries and found their light. Magic and energy, Harbor thought as she and Amethyst glided through the lobby and into the grand ballroom.

The old chandelier was lit, the sea glass casting shards of colored light onto the dance floor. Desi Murphy played the piano and people were already dancing. Mary Templeton hung tight to Hod as they shuffled about while Archie Murphy glided with Ada Flynn. Amethyst grabbed Frank's hand and tugged him to the floor. He blushed but didn't resist. Ruby found Harbor and led her to a table full of delicious foods: cheese and berries, honeyed bread, smoked fish and capers, and, at the end of the table, a multilayered cake baked fresh that day by Mary Templeton and topped with candied lemons.

"I wish you could have a birthday once a week," Ruby said.

"It would have made our time here much shorter," Harbor replied and popped a strawberry into her mouth.

Queen Coralie stepped into the ballroom from a side door, and a hush fell. She wore a gown of oranges and pinks, a jewel-laden necklace, and her crown of precious stones. Opal Pearl and Sapphire followed behind in their own regal gowns. The sight of Sapphire made Harbor stand straighter. She was the eldest of the sisters, and the most powerful. Her blue dress grazed the floor as she walked, and her gray hair reached for the sky in a tremendous swirl of braids and frizz. She wore her glasses, as always, the ones with multiple lenses that she could flip and switch to see what she needed to see. Around her neck were two more pairs of glasses and a magnifying glass besides. She caught Harbor looking at her, and something like a smile crossed her lips. Harbor relaxed, but only slightly.

Queen Coralie laughed and spread her arms out. "Don't stop the festivities because of me. Harbor, come dance!"

Desi switched to a faster tune as Harbor ran to her mother, and the two spun about the dance floor at such a pace that Harbor lost all sense of where she was. All she saw was her mother's sparkling eyes.

Next year would be her last Small Island birthday party, and, Harbor imagined, it would have a different tone altogether. She determined she would have the most wonderful time ever on this night. She danced with her mother and Amethyst and even Frank, who was not much of a dancer, but could spin her high into the air.

When the dancing was done, they ate a decadent meal, and then it was time for the gifts. A chair was brought to the center of the room, simple and wooden. Harbor sat and her aunts stood before her. The people of Small Island watched as each aunt bestowed her gift on Harbor.

"On this night, which marks your twelfth cycle round the sun," Amethyst began, "I bless you with two new freckles on your nose." Amethyst reached out and touched Harbor's face.

Harbor felt two hot stabs. "Amethyst!"

"There you are," Amethyst said. "Now you are perfectly symmetrical. It's been bothering me for ages."

Sapphire gave a disappointed shake of her head, but Harbor didn't care. "Thank you, Amethyst," she said, and gave her aunt a kiss on the cheek. "Though I was quite hoping to be a cat for the night."

"Perhaps next year," Amethyst told her. "I will have to practice mightily for such a transformative feat."

Ruby stepped forward next. She glanced at Sapphire who gave her a sharp nod. Ruby sighed. "On this night, which marks your twelfth cycle round the sun," she said, "I bless you with . . ." She paused. Sapphire raised an eyebrow. "My blessing is that, though you may fall, you will always get up and keep going."

"Persistence," Sapphire said.

"Yes," Ruby said. "For your twelfth birthday, my blessing for you is persistence, so that though you may fall, you will rise and keep going."

Harbor wasn't sure what this blessing meant or why Ruby seemed so reluctant to give it. It was clear she had received a direction from Sapphire, but why?

Harbor's mother cleared her throat.

"Thank you, Ruby," Harbor told her aunt.

Opal Pearl stepped forward next. "On this night, which marks your twelfth cycle round the sun, I bless you with a dash of reason."

"Reason?" Harbor asked.

"So you might think a moment before you act and see the best path." Opal Pearl touched Harbor's forehead.

Finally, it was Sapphire's turn. Harbor's body stiffened. Her aunt peered at Harbor through her glasses, then switched the lenses and peered deeper still. What was she looking for? What did she see?

Sapphire, satisfied, clasped her hands together and tilted her head toward Harbor. "On this night, which marks your twelfth cycle round the sun, I bless you with this ounce of bravery," Sapphire said. She touched her finger to Harbor's chest, and warmth spread over her. "Just in case."

"In case of what?" Harbor asked.

"Life can take strange turns," Sapphire said. "And though I gave you courage at your christening, extra bravery is always welcome, for yourself or to share with others."

Harbor wasn't sure what to make of this. Usually, her aunts

gave her silly blessings, like the extra freckles from Amethyst, but the other sisters seemed far more serious. She frowned, but her mother said, "Harbor," in a tone that Harbor knew meant she was supposed to say thank you. She did but was left with a strange feeling.

Before she could dwell on it too long, Opal Pearl clapped her hands together and said, "Shall we move outside?"

The crowd went all at once, laughing together. As they stepped out into the cool darkness, each person picked up a candle and they made their way to the rocky beach near the dock. It was the most beautiful night Harbor had ever seen. Her friends from Small Island sat on blankets ready for the show.

Only Frank stood apart. He leaned against a pylon of the dock. He watched with a serious face, and she wondered what was bothering him.

Sapphire stood at the edge of the sea, the moon turning her into a silhouette. The other aunts came up behind her and put their hands on her shoulders.

Sapphire placed her glasses over her eyes. She flipped and switched the lenses so one was red and one was black. She looked to the sky, to the sea, and to the land. Once she had her vision, she touched Opal Pearl's chest.

Opal Pearl nodded. She reached out both hands, fingers pointing down. She hummed and pulled tiny drops from the sea and suspended them in the air. They hung like a field full of fireflies frozen in time.

Sapphire touched Ruby's shoulder. Ruby smiled. She

reached toward the honeysuckle flowers and spun her hands. Mist sparkled and danced away from the night blooms.

Next, Sapphire clasped Amethyst's hand. Amethyst, though, already knew her job. She added color to the bubbles: pinks and blues and greens so the night was lit up like a rainbow.

Finally, Sapphire tapped her youngest sister, Queen Coralie. Coralie hugged Harbor tight, and, with her body pressed still against Harbor's, she swirled her hands.

The people gasped. More and more and more drops filled the sky. The drops captured the light of the moon and sparkled with their magic. It was as though the whole town were lifted into the stars.

By his pylon, Frank looked skyward, his face gleaming beneath the light. The others, too, they all looked up. Waiting.

Harbor ran to one drop and touched it with her finger. It popped like a bubble. From it burst the sweet scent of the honeysuckle and the feeling of pure love. She ran from one to the next. She popped them one after the other until she was as wet and salty as if she'd gone swimming.

Everyone watched her: the island's only child playing in the moonlight.

PART TWO

CHAPTER NINE

Two days after her birthday, Harbor slept late. By the time Harbor got to The Place Where Things Wash Up, Mr. Coffin was already coming up the path. "Not much there today," he said.

But Harbor went anyway. As she turned the last corner in the path and the shore came into view, she thought she saw a figure at the edge of the water. It was a person-shaped gray smudge that disappeared almost as soon as Harbor noticed it.

She spotted the sparkling item as soon as she stepped into the water: a unicorn with a horn made of multicolored gems. The unicorn itself was the shimmering white of pearl or opal, the horn purple amethyst, the eyes green stone, and the mane a mix of red rubies and blue sapphires. How strange it was the colors of her aunts' gem names. She reached into the shallow water and pulled it out.

She felt the prick at once.

She looked at her finger, and there it was: a single drop of blood.

The unicorn was attached to a straight pin. When she had grabbed the pin, it pricked her.

So, she thought. *This is it.*

She dropped the pin into her pocket.

She hushed.

She stilled.

The deep, deep sleep she had dreaded for so long suddenly didn't seem so dreadful. It called to her sweetly. She wasn't sure she'd ever felt quite so tired. Just as she was falling asleep, she saw the figure again: a woman with a silver-gray cloak and deep gray eyes.

But perhaps that was a part of the dream she was entering. The mist around the island curled itself into tight clouds that puffed away across the sea. She could see the world beyond: The Somewhere Else. She was in a little skiff—rowing, rowing, rowing on and on toward the horizon. A boy sat beside her. She felt she knew him. They rowed together toward the setting sun. Waspgulls danced above their heads, more than Harbor had ever seen. They rowed and rowed until they were swallowed by the light on the horizon.

Then, she was awake.

At least, she thought she was.

She was in her bed in the cottage with her white sheet and patchwork quilt drawn to her chin. Instead of the dress she'd been wearing that morning, she was in her nightgown. Both her dress and her apron were nowhere to be seen. She had sweat in her sleep and her skin felt sticky.

The light had changed. Instead of the bright sun of midday, it was the cool gloaming of the evening.

Which evening?

Before you reach age thirteen,
With languid limbs and eyes of green,
Something strange, something new,
You'll prick your skin as bright as dew.
A single drop of blood will fall,
A single tear you'll shed.
And by the time the tears have dried,
You may all be dead.

Had hours passed or hundreds of years? She touched her cheeks but felt neither wrinkles nor teardrops. Did that mean everyone was dead?

A drop of blood, sleep will descend,
A hero rises to bring war's end,
A stranger comes from far away,
Fights death and brings a golden day.

Could it be that a whole war had been fought while she slept? The sky was tinged with gold as the light faded from the sky. If so, what did that mean for her? Was everyone else gone, and she the only survivor? Was her mother gone? She clutched her hand to her chest. Her heart thrummed so fast she thought it might jump out. She wanted to call for her mother, but her voice stuck in her throat.

She thought of her father, so steady and brave. He would not stay hidden under the covers. Nor should she.

Shaking, Harbor swung her legs out of her bed. If she had slept a hundred years, what might have happened to her muscles? She sat on the edge of her bed, very still. She was drowsy but felt well rested. She rubbed her eyes. She wondered if her legs would work.

They did.

She blinked.

The room was just as she left it. No dust. No ivy over the windows. And, yes, there on her bookshelf were Lucretia and Sweetwater who stared at her with bright eyes. "What day is it?" she asked the dolls. "What year?"

But of course, the dolls didn't answer because dolls don't speak.

Instead, there was Frank, leaning in the doorway. "It's Thursday. Same as it was this morning."

Harbor leapt into Frank's arms. He pulled her close to him. "Got them all thinking the end of days is coming, you do," he told her. "But I knew this was just a little nap."

Harbor pulled her head back to look at him. She was surprised to see tears in his eyes.

"Is everyone okay?" she asked.

"Right as rain. Just frightened to bits. I was scared, too," he said.

"You?"

"I learned a long time ago that magic has a mind of its own. Blessing or curse, you can't trust it. It's never quite what it seems."

Thoughts of magic brought her mind back to her family. "Where are my aunts?"

"They're all down at the hotel, having their meeting."

"My mother, too?"

"She didn't want to leave you, but I promised to stay right by your door. They don't much listen to me at those meetings, and anyway it would give me a chance to work on my carving." Still holding her in his arms, he reached into the pocket of his dungarees and pulled out a block of wood. "It's going to be a waspgull. I hope. I've tried more'un once and never can get the beak right."

Harbor squeezed herself into Frank so her face was right against his neck.

"Don't you go getting your snot on me, little girl," he told her.

Harbor sniffled in, and Frank let her down to the floor. "What shall we do while we wait for them?" he asked. "Play some checkers?"

As they played the game, she was quite certain he was letting her win. He missed an opportunity to become a king and left himself open for her to jump him three times. It made the game far less fun.

"A pin, was it?" he asked.

"A pin with a unicorn all made of stones. All I saw was the head. I didn't see the pin."

"No one blames you," he told her.

She hadn't been worried about that, though. She was thinking about the pin and the dress she'd been wearing. She was certain she had dropped the pin into the pocket of her apron, so where was it now? And what of that woman she had thought she had seen?

The red spot on her finger seemed smaller. She ran her finger over it. It was hard like a jewel.

"Anyway," Frank went on. "This moment is what we've all been waiting for. It's a bit of a relief if I'm being honest. Now I can teach you how to carve for certain. And you can take your turn baiting the hooks and pulling the fish from the lines 'stead of letting me do all the work."

Harbor wasn't sure if this was true. That was the problem with curses and blessings given in verse: they were never entirely clear, always open to interpretation and misinterpretation. Maybe they had escaped the worst of things, or maybe the war and the hero and the death were still on their way. She wished her aunts had just spoken plainly, especially Micah. If you see fit to curse someone, at least make it a clear one.

When her mother returned several hours later, she didn't give them any answers. She kissed Harbor on the head and thanked Frank for watching over Harbor. Frank left with a nod.

The sleep after the prick had been so deep Harbor felt she might never need to sleep again. Coralie came and sat on her bedside. She brushed Harbor's hair from her face. "I've never been so frightened in all my days," she said.

"And now?" Harbor asked.

"Now I am relieved. But still frightened. We've sent word to your father. Sapphire thinks it best if we go about our lives as normal for now. We must wait and see what comes next."

"Waiting is hard," Harbor said.

"It always is."

"But this is different. Waiting for something good is hard because you want the good thing to come as quickly as possible. Like a birthday. But this, we don't know what it will be or if it will come at all, but it is most assuredly bad." Her stomach twisted as she spoke. "I don't like this feeling at all."

Coralie lay down beside Harbor on the narrow bed. She took Harbor's hand in hers. "Whatever comes, I will be here with you."

The words were a balm and Harbor's body relaxed. As long as her mother was with her, all would be well. Slowly, she drifted into sleep.

In the morning, Harbor woke and went to The Place Where Things Wash Up. Just like always. Sapphire had said they should keep to their normal routines. What she found there was as far from normal as could be.

CHAPTER TEN

The boy sat on the beach with the waves lapping over his toes. His hair, dark brown, was wet, and the locks had lashed across his face and stuck there like mud. His even gaze kept Harbor frozen at the edge of the path.

Mr. Coffin arrived just behind Harbor. He, too, froze.

Harbor thought the boy was younger than her, but she couldn't be sure because she had never met another child. He was certainly smaller than her, nearly half as tall, and his face was rounder. He had wide, bright eyes. His skin was pale white, almost as pale as Mr. Broom's.

"Say something to him," Mr. Coffin whispered.

"Why me?" Harbor asked.

"Because you're a child, too."

The child's lower lip began to quiver. Harbor felt a tug at her gut. She stepped forward. "Hello," she said. "My name is Harbor."

The boy bit on his lip to stop himself from crying.

Harbor crouched. The boy lurched toward her, wrapped his arms and legs around her, and squeezed her tight.

"Welcome to our island," Harbor said. Mr. Coffin nodded at her with something like encouragement. Harbor stood and headed up the path, still carrying the child. Mr. Coffin went in the other direction, toward the village to let everyone know of this strange occurrence.

The boy didn't make a sound. His chest rose and fell against hers, and his breath was hot on her neck. By the time they reached the cottage, her arms felt ready to fall off and her own breath came in heavy gasps.

Her mother stepped out the front door of the cottage at the very moment Harbor and the boy arrived. She dropped her glass of water on the stone steps.

The glass shattered. Water splashed over the steps and onto her mother's dress. The sun glinted off the water and the glass, making tiny rainbows that dissipated almost as quickly as they appeared.

"I found him in The Place Where Things Wash Up," Harbor said.

"Oh," her mother said. Then, because she had no other words, she said it again: "Oh."

Harbor took a step forward, but her mother said, "Stay there, there's glass." She crouched and began picking up the larger pieces. Then, as if noticing for the first time that the boy was soaking wet, she said, "What am I thinking? Come around the back. I'll fetch a towel."

Ten minutes later, the child was wearing some of Harbor's

old clothes and sitting in front of the cook stove. He held tight to Harbor's doll, Lucretia. They all stared at one another: Harbor, the child, and Harbor's mother. None of them could think of what to say.

Finally, Harbor's mother cleared her throat. "We're so happy you've come to Small Island. It is a part of The Lands of Lapistyr."

"Mother!" They weren't supposed to tell outsiders about Lapistyr.

The boy seemed ready to say something, but then all at once the room filled with people: Ruby, Amethyst, Opal Pearl, and all the Murphys. Brigid regarded the boy and gave a sniff. "Doesn't look like much of a hero."

Ruby's blessing danced through Harbor's mind: *a hero rises . . . a stranger comes.*

She had pricked her finger. She had slept. Now here was this stranger—but Brigid was right. He was only a small boy. He couldn't possibly be the hero meant to fight death and bring a golden day, could he?

"He's very sweet-looking," Ruby said, uncertainty in her voice.

"And very small," Archie Murphy added.

All eyes turned to the boy. If he was meant to be their hero, something was very much amiss.

Amethyst twisted her fingers together. It was, after all, her blessing. She always knew it had been hasty, but in that moment she wished more deeply than she ever had that she had spent more time on it, been more specific.

Voices tumbled over one another.

"I suppose he might not be the hero."

"You think it's just a coincidence?"

"Stranger things—"

"But Amethyst's blessing—"

"Well, take into account—"

Queen Coralie patted her sister on the shoulder. "It's not your fault," she said.

"Sapphire will know what to do," Opal Pearl added.

"Yes," the crowd murmured. Sapphire would know. They had to wait for Sapphire.

The boy, who was now practically glued to Harbor, had tears in his eyes and a wavering chin. He surely felt all the eyes on him and heard the skepticism in their voices. His lip quivered harder, and the tears started to spill down his cheeks.

"I think he should like some fresh air," Amethyst said.

Opal Pearl agreed. "Harbor, why don't you show him the island."

"But don't lose him," Ruby said, and gave a nervous laugh. "Stick to the paths."

Harbor nodded. "Okay then," she said to the boy. "Let's go see the island."

He didn't move at first, so she gave a gentle tug at his hand. They left together with the whole room murmuring behind them.

She led him by the hand back out of the cottage to the large boulder that sat in their backyard. Together they scrambled up it, and she gestured toward the ocean. The water glittered like diamonds and filled the air with the smell of salt.

The boy breathed in deeply. He held stiller than Harbor ever knew a person could be. "My name is Peter."

"It's a pleasure to meet you, Peter," she said.

For some reason, this made him laugh. She liked his laugh: it was like the plovers calling to one another.

"I'm from Kansas," he said. "I have a mother and a father, and my mom has a baby in her belly. I hope it's a boy. I want to name him Rex. A girl could be okay, too. If she were like her," he said and shook Lucretia in his hand. "If she were like Lady Luck, all brave and stuff, that might be okay."

"I don't know who Lady Luck is," Harbor said.

Peter shook Lucretia again. "This is Lady Luck, silly. Did you see the one where, like, she, well, it was the one with the Silver Squad? You know, Anvil's minions? He was on vacation, I think. So the Silver Squad was left alone, and they wanted to do bad stuff? Anyway, Lady Luck picked that whole building up? That's my favorite one. Is this a magical island?"

Harbor didn't think she should tell him about her aunts' magic, but his eyes were so hopeful she had to tell him something. So, she told him a story Frank had told her. "Oh, yes," she said. "At least, it used to be back when giants lived here."

"Giants?"

"A peculiar kind of giant," she told him. "They lived in tunnels below the earth and built towers through the ground to the surface. Sometimes you can still find the Giants' Staircases in the wood."

"I don't know if I would like to see a giant. I think I'd like a different kind of magic."

"They're all gone now. You're perfectly safe here."

He sat on the rock. "Do you think I'll ever get home?"

"I'm certain you will," Harbor said, though she wasn't certain at all. She felt bad about lying to him, but his face was so wide and open, his pink cheeks dotted with freckles, his brown eyes so wonderfully warm, she didn't think she could bear to see him cry again. "In the meantime, you'll stay with me, and we shall be the best of friends. I've never had a friend close to my own age before," she confessed.

"The other kids don't like you?" he asked.

Harbor laughed. "No, silly. There are no other kids on this island. Just me. And now you."

The boy reached out his hand and tucked it back into hers. "Then we've gotta be true-blue friends."

A shape emerged on the water. As it came closer, the shape became clearer: a small skiff with two on board. It was coming from the direction of the lighthouse.

"That's Sapphire," she said. "She's one of my aunts." Harbor shuddered.

"Don't you like her?" Peter asked.

"I do," Harbor said. "Of course I do . . ." Harbor wasn't

sure if she could explain how she felt about Sapphire to Peter. She did love her aunt, but Sapphire intimidated her. Whenever she was around, Harbor felt like she was doing everything just a little bit wrong.

"My aunt smells like Pine-Sol," Peter told her. "And we aren't allowed to sit on her couch."

She led Peter through town, past the library to the cliffs that ringed the southeastern corner of the island and the tree that grew clinging to the cliff.

"This is our plumrose tree," Harbor said. The tree was large, with a trunk too wide for Harbor or Peter to hug their arms around, even if they linked their hands. The bark was white, thick, and rough. The leaves, dark green on one side and light on the other, were the shape of hearts. Buried among the leaves were the plumrose fruits. A few lingering blossoms, shaped like delicate pink bells, clung to the limbs.

"There's only three of these trees in all the world," Harbor explained. "One here, one on Lapistyr, and one in the Kingdom of Benspeir. That's my father's kingdom. Some call it The Kingdom of the Clouds or The Kingdom on the Peak. It's on a mountain so high it's above the sky."

She reached up and plucked two fruits from the low-hanging branches.

"There were a different people there before, but they were cursed to live as birds. Some of the birds are still there. They live in these trees and eat the fruits." She handed a plumrose fruit to him. "You can eat it, too."

She showed him how to split the fruit in two and pull

out the seeds. "Ruby would be mad if she saw us wasting these seeds," Harbor said. She gathered them and put them in the pocket of her apron. Ruby used the seeds, as well as the leaves and the bark, in her tinctures and teas.

Harbor watched Peter's face as he took a bite. "It's like a tomato!" he said. "But also a peach—or a plum. A tomato-plum!" The delight spread over his rosy cheeks. Harbor wondered if all young children were so easily pleased. It made her feel warm to watch him smile, and she wondered what else she could show him.

It also made her see Small Island in a new way. In under a year, she'd be gone from this place. Lapistyr had cliffs and the sea and its own plumrose tree, but it would not be this tree, this sea, or this cliff. Nor would it have her library or the Murphy Hotel.

They walked to the rocks and the tide pools where he was awed by the crabs and barnacles and mussels that lived there. Harbor taught him how to hum to make the snails come out of their shells. He squealed with delight.

They watched a seagull snatch a clam and drop it against the rocks to break its shell to eat it.

Peter squished his toes into the sand. Harbor led him to the waterline, and they stood together as the waves came in, their feet sinking deeper and deeper into the sand.

Out in the sea, a seal barked and Peter clapped his hands together. "Some seals can hold their breath for up to two hours," he told her. "Seal pups have a call that their mother can hear for miles."

Harbor was impressed he knew so much about seals.

"I learned it from *Betty and Bo*. Do you watch them? I used to. We had a free trial for the Wild channel. It was like two weeks or two months. Two weeks, I think. Then we stopped it. My mom and dad said we had to save money. I wish I could watch *Betty and Bo* again."

Harbor couldn't understand half of what Peter was talking about, but she liked listening to him. It was lovely to have another child there, especially a younger one filled with so much delight.

Harbor took a stick and wrote in the sand:

Peter and Harbor, True Blue Friends

"Read that to me," Peter said. So, she did. Peter put his hand on his heart. "I solemnly swear," he said. He reached out his pinky to her. He curled it around hers and gave it a shake.

"What's that about?" she asked.

"A pinky promise is the most solemn promise you can make," he said, his voice serious. "And I pinky promise to always be your true-blue friend."

"I promise as well."

Just then, a high whistle called them. It came not from the cottage but the village. They ran together, holding hands.

≈≈≈

Somber faces greeted Harbor and Peter when they entered the lobby of the hotel. Sapphire, Opal Pearl, Ruby, Amethyst, and Coralie stood in a cluster with Leo Murphy close by. Mr. Coffin stood near the stairs, and Frank stood at the door, as if guarding it.

Sapphire crouched before Peter. "How old are you, child?"

"Six," Peter answered.

"Six won't do at all," Sapphire said. "Where is your home?"

"Five oh four Hall Street, Spearville, Kansas," he recited.

"Kansas!" Mr. Coffin cried out. Sapphire silenced him with a glance. She rose back to her full height. Harbor took Peter's hand in hers. The aunts and her mother looked at them with sad faces, all except Amethyst, who turned away.

"It's clear what we must do," Sapphire said.

Mr. Coffin stepped forward. "If he's from Kansas, that means—"

"I know what it means," Sapphire snapped.

Amethyst, who had moved closer to Harbor, whispered, "It means he's from The Somewhere Else."

Everything in Harbor's body trembled.

From the doorway, Frank cleared his throat. "Your Majesty," he said to the queen. When he used the royal address with Queen Coralie, it was not with the friendly, joking tone he used with Harbor. There was an edge to it. "I think what us islanders are concerned about, Queen Coralie, is what that protection will look like. This is our island, our home. We gave up more than we can say in order to stay here."

Frank stepped forward. "If this boy has crossed over, then we aren't so cut off and hidden as we thought. Now it seems there's a war on the way. Just what you promised you'd hide us from." He nodded and then said, again, "Your Majesty."

"We promised protection," Queen Coralie said again. "Lapistyr does not break its promises."

Mr. Coffin scoffed. Harbor felt her cheeks burn. How dare he!

Queen Coralie stepped toward Mr. Coffin, her hands outstretched. "We know sacrifices have been made on this island. That is why we will honor our word. More than our promises, it is this bond of sacrifice that will keep us true."

"That little boy is what you are going to offer in the way of protection?" Mr. Coffin asked.

Sapphire held up her hand. "Amethyst's words promised a hero would rise after Harbor's fall. If this is our hero, he is but a child. He is not ready yet."

Ruby tousled the boy's hair. "A brave hero he will surely one day be."

"There's so much we don't know," Amethyst said. "If we kept him here, at least we would know where he is."

Sapphire glared at her sister. "Perhaps, then, you should have made your blessing clearer. As it is, this boy must return to his home for the time being."

"You can't!" Harbor cried. "He only just got here!"

Peter watched it all wide-eyed.

"It isn't fair, Harbor," Ruby said quietly. "This child needs to be with his family until he's ready to—"

"But what about me?" Harbor demanded, stamping her foot.

Queen Coralie raised an eyebrow at her daughter in the silent way that mothers mind their children. Harbor knew she should let it go, that the grown-ups had made their decision, but she couldn't stop her body from quivering with anger.

Opal Pearl crouched in front of Harbor. "He'll be back, Harbor. I promise. He'll be back when the time is ripe."

"Why can't he grow up here? I've never had a friend. And you are going to rip him away from me—"

Harbor didn't notice Peter's lower lip quivering.

"I ought to have some say. I ought to have some power. What's the point of being a princess if you can't order people to stay!"

Her voice cracked as she yelled. Her mother crossed the room and placed her hands on Harbor's shoulders. "A ruler does what's best for the realm, not what's best for her."

"But it is what's best! He's our hero!"

At that, Peter burst into tears.

Ruby wrapped him in her cloaks. "Oh dear," she said. "Oh dear, dear, dear."

Peter looked right at Harbor. "I do want to go home. I want to see my family."

Harbor sniffled, trying to stop her own tears from flowing. He probably had lots of friends at home. Gobs and gobs of them. He didn't need her.

She spun on her heel and ran out of the hotel.

No one followed her.

So it was that she sat perched on the highest rock and watched as Peter was loaded into a small boat and sent out into a mist that grew up around the island.

As the tiny boat disappeared, Harbor jumped to her feet. "Goodbye!" she yelled. "Come back!"

Perhaps it was just the wind, or a passing bird, but she heard the words "Pinky promise!" drift back over the sea to her.

CHAPTER ELEVEN

Never in her life had Harbor felt so lonely.

She read poems with Amethyst without expression. Even Mr. Broom was disappointed in her performances. He drifted off to sleep, murmuring about elephants and blueberries.

She crushed the herbs and blooms between her fingers as she picked them for Ruby. She didn't even look out for gullsbane.

She painted reddish blobs on canvas and called them plumrose blossoms.

Leo Murphy called her manners absolutely beastly.

With Brigid, her anger found a place. She shot arrow after arrow at the targets Brigid set up for her. She missed her target even more than usual, but the sting of the string felt good. She didn't care that the arrows flew as wild as dandelion seeds.

In their fencing lesson, the two parried back and forth,

grunting with their thrusts. Brigid left an opening. Harbor advanced so quickly that Brigid fell. Her braid swung over her shoulder and *thunked* the ground.

"Ha!" Harbor said.

Brigid was on her feet in a second, her foil pressed right against Harbor's chest.

"You let your guard down, Princess," Brigid growled.

Harbor scowled. "I knocked you over," Harbor said. Even a year ago, she wouldn't have been strong enough to do that. Brigid ought to give her a little bit of credit.

"I understand why you're angry," Brigid said, lowering her foil. "I'm angry, too. Anger can be useful in a duel. But not if the red rage blinds you. Not if you point it in the wrong direction."

Harbor squinted against the bright sun. No one understood what it was like to have a friend for a day only to lose him again.

The two reset. Harbor took a deep breath.

This time, Harbor advanced and retreated. She dodged and held off Brigid's attacks until she saw her moment. Brigid's free hand was above her head, her whole left side exposed. Harbor feigned to her left and then jabbed right into Brigid's abdomen.

Brigid, always dramatic, clutched her side, moaned, fell to the ground, and said, "Harbor, you hath slain me."

The two used their hands to scoop cool water from the fountain outside the hotel into their mouths. "You certainly have people talking, I'll give you that much," Brigid said. "Who was the boy and why was he so young and where did that pin come from? Questions are buzzing around here like flies."

"What do my aunts say?"

"No one dares ask them," Brigid said. "They will tell us what we need to know."

"They ought to tell me, though," Harbor said.

Brigid raised her eyebrows. "You're just a child yourself."

"But I'm the princess!"

Brigid smiled at her. "So you are."

They sat side by side on the edge of the fountain. "Do you really think Peter will return?" Harbor asked.

Beads of sweat dotted Brigid's freckled nose. "I do," she said. "Your aunts said he would."

They hadn't said that precisely. They'd said he was too young, which implied that he would be the right age someday. "But when?" Harbor asked.

Brigid shook her head. "There's no way of knowing. A door was opened and he came through. Who knows when that door will open again?"

Heavy footsteps fell on the veranda of the hotel. "Brigid Murphy and Harbor Rose, you get off that fountain right now!"

Brigid jumped off, but Harbor stayed put, her mind spinning.

A door was opened.

A sentence like that left out who had opened it and how. But Harbor knew: *she* had opened it by being pricked by the pin. If she could find the pin, she could open the door again.

CHAPTER TWELVE

Harbor had always thought of the library as a dignified building. Built of brick with two strong columns beside the front door, it welcomed in readers and information-seekers. She was, indeed, a seeker of information, but now the library loomed ominously.

Harbor hadn't been sure where to start her search for the pin. There were so many places her aunts might hide it. The library had always been where she'd gone to find answers, and Amethyst did always tell her more than the other aunts. It had seemed the logical place to begin, but now that she stood on the steps, she was filled with dread.

She pulled open the door. Amethyst sat on the circulation desk as usual, eating from a bowl of blueberries. As Harbor entered the building, Amethyst leapt to meet her and dragged her through the library, past Mr. Broom who was reading his books and past Ada Flynn who was looking at books on sewing, to a study carrel jammed into a far corner of the library.

"I knew you'd come to me," Amethyst said. "Or, at least, I hoped you would. You must have so many questions."

"And you have books," Harbor said. In the study carrel were two large stacks of books.

"I do," Amethyst said. She pulled out the chair and Harbor sat. "Sometimes it feels books are all I have to offer you. I've tried to give you bits and morsels without breaking any of the rules that Sapphire set. I suppose the pieces don't make much sense without the whole story." Amethyst leaned against the carrel and sighed. She rubbed her hand over her hair and turned it deep brown. "What I mean to say is, I understand your curiosity and I want to show you something."

Amethyst touched her hair again. She turned it a purple gray, then soft silver, then golden. "I'm sorry," she said. "Nothing seems just right for this moment." She took a clip from her own hair and placed it into Harbor's. She paced. She clutched her pale pink dress and turned it pine green. "Better," she said. Then she flopped into a leather armchair near the study carrel. Her feet were bare, and she tucked them under her. Finally, she said, "Tell me what you think The Somewhere Else is."

"It's faraway places. Unexplored places," Harbor said. "When things wash up, they come from The Somewhere Else." As she spoke, she realized how flimsy her understanding was. She had assumed that The Somewhere Else was someplace on the other side of the globe, too far away to be explored. People couldn't make the journey, only things, tossed and worn by the sea. Peter was the first person to wash up, but that was because of magic. But perhaps there was something more to it. "I guess I'm not sure. No one ever talks about it in any detail."

Amethyst sucked her cheeks in. "It's never been forbidden, precisely," she said, more to herself than Harbor.

"What?" Harbor demanded. Even as she asked, she felt the sickness of dread in her stomach.

Amethyst opened the atlas. "This map shows The Somewhere Else. One of them. Peter's Somewhere Else."

Harbor looked at the map. None of it looked familiar. "Where is Benspeir? Where are we?"

Amethyst took a plain piece of paper. She held it until it turned translucent as tracing paper. She carefully placed the paper on top of the world map. With a library pencil, she drew other shapes, shapes that were familiar to Harbor: Benspeir, Lapistyr, the great Soth lands, the vast expanse to the west that they called The Doldrums. "This is our world," Amethyst said. "Our map." She slid the paper away and pointed to the book. "This is theirs."

Harbor didn't understand what her aunt was trying to tell her. "Think of it as layers, worlds on top of worlds. Or beside. Directionality was never my strong suit, especially when it comes to The Many Realms."

"That makes no sense. Things wash up here. They don't drop from the sky. Peter didn't drop from the sky or ooze from the ground."

"I know it's confusing. When we learned about it in school, I needed Micah to explain it to me again and again. Of course, it makes sense to her. Micah is all layers, like glass. We are here, and they are The Somewhere Else. Alike, but not." As she spoke, she held out one hand, palm down. She placed the other hand on top of it, a small space between. "Like fog," Amethyst said. "Sometimes, in some places, the fog touches the lands in all the layers. In those places, sometimes, the worlds can blend." She pressed on the paper, and the space under her finger began to blend into the map below.

"Like in Kansas?"

"Apparently," Amethyst said. "We've worked so hard to keep ourselves hidden perhaps we've neglected to understand the way our worlds are intertwined."

Amethyst turned to a map labeled *North America*. "There," she said, and pointed at a square-shaped space right in the middle of a vast area marked as *United States of America*.

"Kansas," Harbor said out loud. It was as far from the ocean as it could be. How sad for Peter.

Amethyst drew her finger along the map in a gentle arc eastward and northward from Kansas. She stopped at a strangely shaped block marked *Maine*. Then she slid her finger just a little more east, out into the ocean. With the pencil, she made a small X. "Dirigo," she said.

Harbor's head spun. "Are you saying we live in some sort of in-between place?"

"Not precisely," Amethyst said. "We live in a hidden place. Opal Pearl and Sapphire, they're good at hiding things." She paused. "I know what you're looking for, but I cannot tell you where to find it. That much is clear. And, for what it's worth, I agree Peter was too young. We will call him back when he is needed, and hopefully, he will be ready then. In the meantime, you must be patient."

Harbor had never been very good at being patient.

"If I could, I would go there and watch over him for you."

"Why don't you?" Harbor asked.

"I'm not meant to travel there." Amethyst smiled. "I understand your curiosity, though. When I was your age, The Somewhere Else was all I thought about. While Sapphire was studying and Opal Pearl and Ruby were gathering, Micah and I—"

"Micah!" Harbor couldn't help but exclaim. Amethyst had mentioned her earlier in the conversation. It was the most anyone had ever spoken of Harbor's wayward aunt.

"We were sisters once. We *are* sisters," Amethyst said. "Thick as thieves, our mother used to say." Amethyst blinked, and Harbor thought she might have seen tears in her aunt's purple eyes.

"Why did she do it, Amethyst? Why did she curse me?"

"I'm not sure. Your father thought it was because they hadn't invited her to the christening, but Micah was never one for parties. Aside from the food. She loved the food. And dancing. But not all the people." Amethyst hesitated. "Things were . . . hard after your parents fell in love. Hard for Micah. She and Coralie had been very close, but there was something else. Micah never trusted the people of Benspeir."

"Why not? And why curse her own lands? Was it just jealousy?"

"She didn't think your father was a good match for your mother."

"He is!" Harbor cried.

"Micah had her own way of looking at things. Always trying to find balance, and something about Benspeir could never be right for her."

Amethyst drew Harbor into her arms. "I'm so terribly sorry she did it. I'm sorry I couldn't fix it properly. I trust you, though, Harbor. I trust you to do what is right." She held Harbor at arm's length. "I told you this because I think you have a right to know."

Amethyst stared meaningfully at Harbor. Harbor wasn't sure what message she was supposed to be receiving.

Amethyst bit her lip. "This is more than I was meant to tell you. We were supposed to wait, but I didn't think you ought to wait anymore. Not after Peter. Not with what's coming. There's so much more you need to know—"

A bell chimed at the front of the library. Amethyst let her hands drop off Harbor's shoulders. "Drat," she said. "I have to go see to my patrons. Please, trust my sisters. They know best how to protect you—how to protect us all. When the time is right, you'll know everything. Until then: trust."

Harbor nodded and watched Amethyst go in a swirl of colors.

Secrets.

Why were her aunts keeping so many secrets from her?

CHAPTER THIRTEEN

The fish were not biting for Harbor and Frank. They sat with their feet hanging off the edge of the dock and let the sun warm them.

"What did you mean when you said you were promised protection?"

Frank rubbed his head. "We'd protect you and they'd protect us. It was a deal we made."

"Protect you from what?"

"It was a long, long time ago, Harbor."

"Not that long ago," she said. If she was a Seer, she'd pick a lens and look right at Frank and see what it was he was thinking about. If she had that kind of magic, then she could know the truth.

"Harbor, girl, there are some bears you shouldn't poke."

Harbor laughed. "I don't suppose you should poke any bears." She knew about bears from stories: huge animals with fierce claws that liked to eat blueberries of all things.

She had often hoped to meet a baby one while picking berries, but never had.

"Except for the Pokalot Bear, of course," Frank said.

"What's that?" she asked.

"The Pokalot Bear is the rarest of bears. It lives only in caves of pure quartz and eats only raspberries and lemon cakes."

"Lemon cakes! You're making this up."

"Perhaps I am," he said. "We islanders love a story. Love 'em so much sometimes we walk right into one."

Harbor puzzled over what he said, then realized he had steered her right away from what she had wanted to talk about. "Were you in danger?"

"Of a sort," Frank said. Frank let out a long, low breath. "I never told you about my older brother. Billy was his name. Oh, I idolized him. He was strong and fast and funnier than a son of a gun. Pardon me."

"What did he look like?" she asked. "Was he handsome like you?"

"Now, Harbor, you're going to make me blush. But, yes, he was handsome. All the girls loved him, but he only had eyes for the sea—and for stories. Never met someone who liked stories half as much as he did. Especially stories about far-off places. His favorites were about the brave explorers who went to the place the compass spins."

Harbor tucked herself closer to Frank. She didn't know how this story was going to end, but she knew it would be bad.

"He asked me to come with him, but, well, if I'm being

96

perfectly honest, I was too scared. I like the sea well enough, but I like coming home to land."

"Me too," Harbor agreed. "What happened to him?"

"He's still out there. I hope."

"He never came back?"

"Not yet," Frank said. "That was many years ago. I used to think the magic of this place, the women—I used to think it'd all bring him back."

"When I have my magic—"

"Don't go wishing for things you don't understand."

"But I will understand it once it's mine."

Frank raised his eyebrows. "I'm not so sure anyone truly understands magic, whether they have it or not."

Harbor was about to protest, but Frank cut her off. "What do I know? I'm just a fisherman on one Small Island." He tousled her hair. "Just promise that when you get your magic, you won't forget old Frank."

"Never!" she exclaimed.

A long, low whistle sounded from up the hill. At the end of the dock was Brigid with two ponies.

"Did I make you feel a little better?" Frank asked.

"You did," she replied.

"I'm sorry about that boy. I'm sorry he had to go. Every child deserves a playmate." He rubbed his head again and looked her right in the eye. "I've tried to be a good friend to you, but I'm afraid somewhere along the way I've become a boring old man."

"You're nothing of the sort! You're barely even old at all." Harbor squeezed him into a tight hug.

"Thank you, Sweet Harbor," he told her. "Now you best be off with Brigid. I wouldn't want one of the queen's own soldiers mad at me."

With a wave, Harbor ran up the dock to Brigid so they could do their daily exercises. His sadness clung to her. She would help him someday, she promised herself. When she had her magic, she'd find his brother.

CHAPTER FOURTEEN

If they had asked me," Brigid said from astride her pony, "which they most certainly did not. But if they had asked me, I would have told them to make a lockbox for it. Something strong. Out of metal. Two locks with two separate keys held by two separate people. Then a third person to hide the box. That would keep that pin safe."

Harbor had let slip that the pin was no longer in her possession, taken, she assumed, by her aunts. Brigid had deemed that a good move. "That's a powerful weapon. It's wise to keep it safely tucked away," Brigid told her.

"A weapon?" Harbor asked.

"A tool that can call a great hero from another land? I'd call that a weapon, yes." She stopped her pony and dismounted. They were at the edge of the forest. Shadows loomed, and strange bird calls came from within it. Harbor never went into the woods, not past where Ruby lived. The trees stretched across the island all the way to the cliffs on the other side, and her mother and aunts told her the woods were easy to get lost in and full of wild beasts.

Brigid and Harbor tied their ponies to a tree as Brigid kept talking. "Of course, in an actual emergency, three people might be too many. You'd want two, at least. Perhaps there ought to be two copies of each key and each of your aunts could hold one. Then they'd only need two of the aunts to open the box. Just in case."

Harbor trusted everyone on the island. Even Mr. Coffin, her rival, wouldn't steal something. So, why would they even need to hide the pin away?

Brigid sensed her discomfort. "There's a war coming, Harbor. This isn't a game. I know you were glad to have a child here with you, but that's not his role. Peter's not a friend; he's our hero."

Harbor's canvas shoe had a hole that showed the nail of her big toe. Her knees were skinned. She looked like a ragamuffin, like a little girl. Brigid was right: Harbor wanted Peter to come back to be her friend. She wanted someone to range over the island with, to laugh with. That he was also a hero mattered to Harbor, but his friendship mattered more. To her, war felt far off. Even the whole curse seemed overly dramatic to her, especially now that she'd experienced it. "I understand."

"I'm not sure you do," Brigid said. "But that's not my job. My job is to prepare you for the fight, not to convince you it's coming." Brigid, Harbor knew, was itching for a fight. This post on the island, being Harbor's instructor, might have a certain honor to it, but it wasn't exciting. Harbor assumed that to a true soldier, safety on an island and looking over a child was an embarrassing task, even if that child was a cursed princess.

Brigid took her bow from her back and an arrow from her quiver. She took her stance and squared her body toward the sea. A bale of hay, covered in cloth and riddled with arrow marks, stood at the edge of the cliff. Brigid wanted Harbor to be able to shoot straight even with the sun glaring off the ocean. Archery was Harbor's worst skill, and the glare of the sun only made it worse. Harbor wondered if there was a kind of magic that could help her to shoot straighter.

Brigid notched the arrow, then pulled back the string. She let the arrow fly, and it slammed into the hay.

"If the war is coming, shouldn't we have our hero here? Ready?" Harbor asked.

"He wasn't ready."

"But he won't—"

Brigid took out another arrow. "However, you make a good point."

"I do?"

"I rescind my earlier position and present another. If I were in charge of the unicorn pin, I'd keep it on my person at all times. That way I'd be able to get it to you as soon as we needed it." She shot her second arrow and prepared a third. "Of course, if it were actually me, that would be a terrible choice because you and I spend so much time together and while we were training, you might accidentally prick yourself." She sent her final arrow zinging. The arrows made a perfect triangle. "Your turn. Right in the center."

Harbor placed her feet so they faced the target at the right angle.

"The best person to hold it," Brigid went on, "would be someone close, but not too close."

Harbor notched her round-tipped arrow and raised her bow. She aimed at the target. Beyond the target, beyond the cliffs and out at sea, was the lighthouse where Sapphire lived. She let her arrow fly. It angled to the right, hitting the target but nowhere near the triangle.

"Harbor! That's worse than your usual!"

"Sorry," Harbor said. "I was thinking of something else."

"You must never think of something else while shooting!"

Harbor nodded. "Yes, of course."

All the while she kept her gaze on Sapphire's lighthouse: close, but not too close.

CHAPTER FIFTEEN

Harbor thought she was going to have to use subterfuge to get the little sailboat and go out to see Sapphire, but it was really very easy. In the morning, she said to her mother, "I think I should like to see Sapphire today."

Her mother said, "That sounds like a lovely idea. I'm sure she would be happy for the surprise."

Harbor had been full of excuses and reasons and was, indeed, a little let down by the lack of protest she had received from her mother.

She made her way to the dock where Frank was fixing his lobster traps, and she said, "May I please take the sailboat? I am going to see Sapphire."

Frank told her it was as much her boat as anyone else's and to have a nice trip.

Harbor got into the boat, and Frank helped her to push off. She tested the wind, raised her sail, and set her tiller.

Harbor and the boat were both so small, and yet, together, they were able to harness something as powerful as the wind. It whipped her hair against her face and filled her sails and powered her across the mighty sea.

She kept an eye out for seals. That they could stay underwater for up to two hours was quite impressive. She wondered if Peter had been right, though, about the pup's call to their mother.

Soon the lighthouse was close. She trimmed her sail and aimed for the little dock. As she eased her boat against the wood, Sapphire's face appeared in a window. She didn't look surprised. Nor did she look pleased.

With a sinking feeling in her stomach, Harbor tied her boat, then went inside. Up and up and up the twisting staircase to the room where Sapphire lived. There were boxes and tables filled with books and other trinkets: a hunk of coral, a fist-sized crag of smoky quartz, a monkey's paw knot as big as her head, a glass ball. It was overwhelming. Harbor looked instead toward the windows: three circles, small, medium, and large, all looking out to the sea.

"You have come," Sapphire said. Her face was stern. She stood in the center of the room, still among the chaos. Her faded blue dress brushed the floor. Her thick glasses were nestled in her wild hair, and around her neck was a magnifying glass on a chain. "Welcome." She lifted her magnifying glass to her eye and looked Harbor up and down.

Harbor felt herself grow hot as if Sapphire's eye were the

sun and the glass were setting her on fire. She had always been intimidated by Sapphire, but now that fear was more intense. Her aunts had been keeping secrets from her, and now Harbor had a secret of her own. The feeling was raw and itchy.

Sapphire dropped her lens, and it swung on the chain. "You have come to ask about The Many Realms."

Harbor let her breath out, relieved that Sapphire had not seen that she had come in search of the pin.

Sapphire fingered the magnifying glass. "It is past time for us to explain this to you." She crossed the room and sat in her armchair, picking up her embroidery. She dropped her glasses over her eyes. Sapphire pulled her needle up and down, up and down. Harbor couldn't help but shudder. She had been pricked. She knew what brought on her curse. Still, sharp, pointed objects filled her with fear. Sapphire peered at Harbor over her glasses. The air practically sizzled between them. "Before I answer your questions, I have my own questions for you."

Harbor sat on a footstool near her aunt. She tried to remain calm.

Sapphire stabbed the fabric with her needle and tugged. "Before you pricked your finger, did you notice anything strange?" Sapphire looked through her glasses at her embroidery, but Harbor still felt she was being watched from all angles. Her neck itched, and it was hard to keep still.

"Strange?" Harbor asked. She thought of the person she had dreamed she had seen disappearing into the mist. "No,

I don't think so." She paused. "I did think it strange that the pin had all your stones."

"Our stones?" Sapphire asked.

"Opal, ruby, amethysts, and sapphires. Plus emeralds for the eye."

"Emerald was our mother's stone," Sapphire said.

"It felt like the pin was somehow meant for me."

Sapphire paused in her embroidery. "You saw nothing else? No one else?"

Harbor swallowed hard. "Only Mr. Coffin."

"He was there before you?" Sapphire's fingers began their work again. "And he did not see the pin?"

"I guess not. He is old, you know."

"But still sharp of eye." Sapphire's mouth creased into a frown.

"I had to wade out to find it. It was buried in the sand, only the unicorn itself showing."

"It's not like Mr. Coffin to miss anything." She frowned still deeper and her eyes flashed.

"You don't think he put it there? To prick me?" Harbor asked. The idea felt both right and wrong all at once.

Sapphire barked out a crisp laugh. "He would no sooner harm you than harm his own blood." She placed the embroidery aside. "Very well then. Let us now address your questions about The Many Realms. What do you know, and what do you wish to know?"

Harbor twisted her fingers together. She could not get

this wrong, and she could not expose Amethyst, the only aunt willing to tell her anything at all. "It seems like perhaps the realms are layered on top of each other, but I don't understand how things pass from one world to another."

"How do you pass from one room to another?" Sapphire asked.

"I go through a door," Harbor said.

Sapphire lifted her glasses back into her hair, but she kept her gaze trained on Harbor. "Precisely. Between The Many Realms, there are doors and windows and places where there are no walls at all. Things pass through those doors and windows and wall-less places. Some of those things wash up on Small Island."

"Some people do, too," Harbor said.

"Yes."

"But it doesn't line up precisely. Peter was from Kansas. I saw it on a map. It's far from here."

"Far from *here?*" Sapphire's eyes narrowed.

"Far from the sea," Harbor said quickly, recognizing she had made a mistake. Sapphire was as quick as she was wise and never missed a detail.

"You are thinking of the layering too literally. Our world is not a paper map, is it?"

Harbor shook her head.

"To map The Many Realms and the ways they intersect would take a cartographer of great talent. Instead, we must feel the connections rather than capture them on paper."

"I see," Harbor said, but she did not. "Right here, is it a door or a window or a place with no walls?"

"Again, I fear you are being too literal."

"Peter washed up on the shore, just him. But you sent him back on a boat."

Sapphire frowned. "You ask the right kinds of questions, but these are details you need not worry about. And I fear your motivations. I know you want the boy back. I know you are clever and resourceful. We all realized at once that you would try to find a way to force his return."

Sapphire lowered her glasses and looked at Harbor. Harbor burned.

"That is magic you cannot understand or control. The bringing of someone from one realm to another, that takes powerful magic and great skill."

"But it is my curse."

"No, it is your *blessing*. Amethyst's blessing is what allows the hero to come."

Harbor bit her lip. Amethyst thought her magic was weak and unfocused, but it was her magic that had allowed Harbor to call Peter. Her magic and the pin. The blessing and the curse were as intertwined as the sisters themselves. Harbor wanted to ask Sapphire why Micah would curse them so. Amethyst's response still didn't make sense to Harbor. Sapphire might know more, but Harbor was too afraid to ask.

Sapphire gathered her skirts and walked toward the

windows. She found a stool for Harbor to stand on and asked her to look out the largest window. "What do you see?"

Harbor stood on her tiptoes. She looked past the still water and the shadow of an island in the distance, the one her father called The Nearly There Place, and out toward the distant horizon. "Clouds," she said. "Storm clouds. Only they are not gray. Not precisely."

"What are they then?"

"Silver? And icy. I'm not sure how I can tell that, but they are." She shivered. "They give me the most tremendous sense of cold."

"That is The Frost," she said. "That is our war."

"A frost?" Harbor asked, incredulous.

Sapphire took her hand and Harbor stepped down. "Look through the middle window," Sapphire instructed.

Harbor did as she was told. When she peered through the window, all she saw was silver and white, so bright it nearly burned her eyes. "It's nothing," she said. "Just light and glinting." She pulled back from the window. "What is this glass?"

"Each window is a lens," Sapphire explained. "We never see all of anything we look at with our eyes. We need lenses." She tapped her magnifying glass. "There are lenses for seeing things that are far away in distance and in time and lenses for pulling back on what is close—"

Harbor interrupted, "You're saying you can see the future in these windows? What does this one show?"

"Look closer," Sapphire said.

Harbor leaned in. At first the white-silver light seemed solid and still. Harbor jumped back, nearly knocking into Sapphire. "It's moving!" she cried.

"Look closer," Sapphire said again, her voice still calm.

Harbor leaned in, though she feared what she would see. The movement began to take form. From squiggles and lines, shapes emerged. "Are those . . . people?"

"The Frost are a people of sorts. Perhaps they were once human. Perhaps not. Some say they are descended from those who lived in The Kingdom That Was on Benspeir, before your father's people."

"But they were all turned into waspgulls," Harbor said.

"So the stories say, but that is a history of long ago. Another theory says The Frost are creatures who willed themselves to life in the barren icelands out of loneliness, that they can take any form and choose something human-like to instill fear in their enemies."

"But why do they come for us? Why do they think us their enemies?"

"They come for everyone. They make the people their own. Every land as well. They suck it dry, turn it to ice."

Harbor could picture her island icing over. It made her whole chest feel tight, but Sapphire seemed unbothered. How could she not be terrified? Such a horrible, horrible enemy Micah had sent for them and all because she did not like Coralie's choice for a husband? Her hatred of Benspeir was such that she would freeze over all those she had once

110

loved? Amethyst said that Micah sought balance, but this was wildly out of line with any slight.

"When?" Harbor demanded. "When will they be here?"

"Soon or never. It's hard to say."

Sapphire's calm aggravated Harbor. How could Sapphire not want to call Peter at once, to bring him to this land to protect them? She wasn't sure how such a small boy would be able to save them, but the blessing said a hero would arrive, and if Peter was the hero, then so be it. The storm clouds were forming quickly, doubling as she watched. They needed Peter and they needed him right away.

Harbor pulled back from the window. "Sapphire," she said in a small voice, "we must do something."

"We will," Sapphire said.

"But what?" Harbor demanded. "And when? If The Frost is coming, we must call Peter back. Before it's too late."

Sapphire narrowed her eyes. She spoke in a low voice. "I have been alive for many years and many days. You are but a child. You think you know better than me?"

Harbor felt singed from the inside out. "No, I—"

Sapphire's anger extinguished as quickly as it had flamed. She smiled at Harbor. "It is a large problem, too much for you to bear, little one."

This was a different side of Sapphire, one Harbor was not used to seeing: soft. This scared her more than the crystallized sternness Sapphire usually showed. "I can take it," she said. "It is my duty."

"You rush too quickly without looking," Sapphire said. "It

is done with honor, but is reckless, nonetheless. You need to see better." She cocked her head to the side, as though an idea had just occurred to her. She reached into her pocket and pulled out a very small lens that hung on a chain. The lens was concave in both directions, like a hollow marble, and ringed with brass. The glass itself was not clear but tinted green. She handed it to Harbor who draped it over her neck. "It will help you to better see what you need to see."

"It's lovely," Harbor said. "Thank you."

Sapphire's smile faltered, and then she turned and said, "Let us have some tea. Ruby makes a special batch for me."

Harbor held the lens to her eye at the exact time Sapphire turned. Harbor saw it: the unicorn pin. It was stuck into the collar of Sapphire's dress, under her hair. She moved the lens from her eye. Nothing. But, looking through the rounded glass again, she could see it: Sapphire had hidden the pin beneath her gray hair. Brigid had been right: close, but not too close. Harbor's elation fizzled almost as quickly as it appeared. There was no way she could get that pin from Sapphire's neck.

Think, think, think, Harbor urged herself. Maybe if she spent the night and Sapphire fell asleep, then she could slip the pin from Sapphire's collar. But, while Harbor had slept in Opal Pearl's cottage and Ruby's greenhouse and Amethyst's rooms above the library, she had never once spent the night with Sapphire. Just the thought of it made her squirm. Would Sapphire snore? Would she whisper spells in her sleep?

Sapphire stood on a stool to get a tin of tea leaves. The unicorn pin glinted at her neck.

Perhaps I could just grab it?

Sapphire tensed. She touched her collar next to the pin.

But that was impossible, Harbor thought. *She cannot read inside my mind. Or could she?* Her aunt was distant, mysterious. Perhaps she *could* read inside people's minds. Harbor put her hand over her heart as if Sapphire could read that, too.

As Sapphire filled the teakettle with water and set it on her small stove, Harbor thought and thought and thought, and then it came to her: she did not need to have the pin. She only needed to be pricked.

"Sapphire—" Harbor began. Sapphire turned back to face her. Harbor took a deep breath. "I—I simply—" she stuttered. Then she collapsed in a heap and sobbed.

It was a tremendous performance. Her body shook, and fat tears dropped down her cheeks. Sapphire came at once and crouched beside her. Harbor wrapped her arms around Sapphire's neck.

It was easy to find the pin. Easy to be pricked. Easy to fall asleep.

The easiness would end when she awoke.

CHAPTER SIXTEEN

When Harbor woke in her own bed, Frank was there. "I'm not meant to be nice to you. Not one lick of kindness."

Harbor's mouth was dry, and her head ached. She sat up, and there was Lucretia staring back at her with frozen disappointment.

"What were you thinking?" Frank asked.

"If I could get him back, he could save us," Harbor said.

"He's just a boy. He can't save anyone." He kicked the floor with the toe of his boot. "You've made a real mess of things, Harbor girl."

Harbor felt her heart sink. Still, she had to go. Had to meet Peter. She swung her legs over the side of the bed.

"He didn't show, if that's what you're hoping."

"What? What do you mean?"

"Your boy didn't wash up this time. Least not here. Who knows, maybe he's still floating about the sea."

"No," Harbor said. "No, no, no!" Her mind tumbled as it tried to keep up with what she was learning. Outside, the sun shined brightly. It was morning. Past sunrise. Peter should be here! "I thought—"

"You weren't thinking at all, that's the problem."

Frank had never been angry at her before, not even when she had swamped his skiff and he'd had to bail it out bucket by bucket. But he was mad now. Really mad. "I told you that magic can't be trusted."

"I was trying to help!" she cried. The vision of The Frost was singed in her mind. The fear pressed down at her.

"You don't know what you're messing with. I was once as wide-eyed about magic as you are. When your aunts came, I wasn't much older than you are now, and I thought—" He stopped himself. "You aren't to leave. I'll be outside keeping watch. Your mother and the rest of them are furious, you should know." He left the room and stomped down the stairs.

Harbor flopped back on the bed. No Peter? But she had been pricked. She had slept. It was just like last time.

But it wasn't, she realized. The first time it had been an accident. This time she had done it on purpose. Though she had assumed a cause and effect, that was just a hypothesis. Perhaps the door had not opened for Peter this time. Or perhaps he had gone through and was indeed floating around the ocean. Or washed up somewhere else. Or perhaps someone else entirely had come through.

She *had* made a mess of things. She hated to cry, but sometimes you just needed to, and the tears and the sobs spilled out of her. Amid her tears and sobs, a new sound emerged. A *plink-plink* sound. She sniffled and listened harder.

Plink-plink.

There it was! At her window. She watched and a pebble hit the glass. *Plink!*

She rushed to the window. Down below, by the hedge and barely hidden, squatted a boy about her age, wet to the bone. She stepped back. Who was this boy, and why was he throwing pebbles at her window?

She lifted the sash and leaned out. She held up one finger to the boy. *Quiet*, that finger said. And, *I'll be right down.*

Frank sat on the front steps carving his wooden figures, so she would have to sneak out the back. The good thing was no one ever expected her to disobey, so if Frank told her to stay, he assumed she would stay. She would have if a mysterious boy had not shown up in her hedgerow.

She crept down the stairs, walking on the edge of each tread so as not to make a sound. By the back door, she tugged on her boots, then slipped outside.

"Harbor!" the boy said, stepping away from the hedge.

"Shh!" she whispered back.

She grabbed the boy by the arm and tugged him along the hedge to the back garden where a little gate led them to a path. They followed it up to the cliffs, and then, finally, she turned to face him. He had familiar golden-brown curls and brown eyes. "How do you know my name?" she demanded.

"You're the girl who lives on the island. You're Harbor. I can't believe I'm back here! No one believed me. Everyone thought I was making it up. Well, except for Anna, but she's not quite six."

"Peter?" Harbor had grown up surrounded by things most people would find impossible, but a boy who had aged several years in a matter of days was too much even for her.

"Yes, of course. Who else would it be?" He paused. "Do you invite a whole bunch of kids through the door?"

"No, I—"

"Good, because I really want this to be my special place. Our special place. I'd show Anna if I could, but no one else." He looked around them. "It hasn't changed a bit here. I remember every detail."

"How long has it been since you were here last?" Harbor asked.

"Nearly six years, I guess. I was six then. That made it okay at first. Everyone thought it was a story or a dream, but I kept talking about it. Then one day my father told me to stop. 'You're nearly twelve years old, Peter,' he said. 'You can't be going on about this make-believe fairyland nonsense.' And I did stop talking about it, but I never stopped believing. Of course, it wasn't nonsense because here I am and here you are and—" Peter stopped himself. He looked Harbor up and down. "How come you haven't changed at all?"

"It's hardly been a week," she told him.

"But—" he began.

The two of them stood there, gape-mouthed.

"So the timelines are different," he said. "That makes sense. I mean, I've seen movies like that. So, I guess, well, time moves differently in different places. Different dimensions."

"Dimensions?" she asked. "You mean like The Many Realms?"

"Maybe? I suppose we could call it different things. Like, on my world, we have a whole lot of multiverses. Comics mostly, and the characters exist in different versions and in different timelines. Like Lady Luck. I remember you had that doll. In the main timeline, her alter ego is named Lucy and she works at a bookstore. But in the Silver Timeline, she works in a casino in Berlin in the 1940s and uses the intel she gathers there to take down Nazis. That's my favorite era of the comic. What does she do here?"

"Who?" Harbor asked.

"Lady Luck," he said. "You had her doll. Action figure, really. You called her something else."

"Lucretia?"

"Is that her alter ego name on this world?"

"I—" Harbor began, but she had no words. None of this made any sense, and all of it felt *wrong*. He still felt like Peter, though she couldn't quite place what she meant by that. "I think I made a mistake." She took a deep breath in. She had to stop, slow down, and figure out what was happening

118

before everything spun out of control entirely. "Where did you come from? How did you get to my window?"

Peter grinned. "Oh, right! Well, when I, you know, got here, I was in the water and I could see the shore and I saw people standing there. They were there and then not there and then kind of there but not. But I could tell they were your aunts. And, no offense, but your aunts kind of scare me. So, I dove down and came up on the rocks and then snuck to your house. I'm really good at sneaking. And I remembered where your house was."

"My aunts scare me, too, sometimes," Harbor admitted. "Especially Sapphire. I'm sure they aren't very happy with me for calling you back. But things are happening. I had to do it. I had to."

Peter sighed. "Well, even if we get in all the trouble in the world—in both our worlds—I'm still glad to be here. Glad to be away from stupid Cam Lockhorn."

"Who's Cam Lockhorn?" Harbor asked.

"The worst person ever," Peter said. Then he shook his head and body as if shaking the very idea of this Cam Lockhorn off him. "Anyway, I joined lacrosse. Do you have lacrosse here?" He held his hands to his chest as if holding a staff, but he swiveled his wrists and dodged and weaved like he was dodging blows from a foil.

"No. I don't think we do."

"I play goalie, and I'm pretty great at it. Coach says I'm a beast."

"I saw Kansas," she said. "On a map. You're right. It's very far from the ocean."

"I've been to the ocean now, too!" he said. "My parents took us to North Carolina for a vacation, and we got to go up in this little plane, and we saw these wild horses running around. We stayed in Kitty Hawk. That's where the Wright brothers flew their first plane."

"That sounds nice," she said. When he was talking, Peter was full of his old enthusiasm. When he wasn't talking, though, his shoulders stooped. He held his hands in fists. His eyes didn't flash as bright as they used to.

Just then came the low ringing sound of a bugle. Peter startled. Harbor, though, clapped her hands together. "My father arrives!" she cried. She jumped to her feet. "He will know what to do," she promised. "He will fix everything."

Harbor was certain of this. Fixing things and smoothing them over was what her father did. He would understand why she had felt the need to call Peter, and, even better, her father would know how to protect them all from The Frost.

CHAPTER SEVENTEEN

The ship in the harbor was one of her father's smaller ones with a high bow that held at its point a bright polished sphere of green tourmaline with a carved waspgull sitting atop it. It was the *Downeaster*. A newer, faster ship. Perhaps he had wanted to show her this new ship for her birthday—he always came in her birthday month. A good thing, too. There was much that needed sorting! Harbor turned over her shoulder to Peter. "Hurry!" she cried.

Peter jogged behind her, wary of the crowd forming. He had been treated kindly the last time he had been to the island, but he remembered how quickly he had been ushered away.

The launch boats were already in the water making their way toward shore. Harbor's heart sung. Her father would know what to do. He would know how to stop The Frost. He would not hesitate and hedge as her aunts were doing.

Harbor and Peter reached the dock at the same time as her mother who twisted her hands and didn't remark about the reappearance of the boy at all. Amethyst came to her side. "He is here too quickly," she said. "We only just sent word."

"He's here for my birthday!" Harbor exclaimed.

"However he knew to come, I am relieved he is here."

Amethyst caught Harbor's eye and smiled. That little expression was the final clue Harbor needed. *Everything was going to be okay.*

When the first launch boat reached the dock, Ida, the king's master-at-arms, jumped out first. Her shiny black boots clipped with each step, sharp and official. Her uniform of deep purple leather and wool was decorated with gemstones from Lapistyr. The front of her pants were embroidered with the stories of her military escapades. But it was her headpiece that caught Harbor's eye. The cap was made of the same soft, purple leather as her uniform. A band around her head was completely covered in a mosaic of gemstones. Hidden among them, Harbor knew, was a small piece of shell given to Ida by Brigid. Ida's hair, dark and curly, spilled out from beneath the cap like a crown. All the soldiers wore this uniform, but Harbor was certain that no one looked as powerful in it as Ida.

Behind Ida came a score of foot soldiers, each dressed in similar uniforms, though none so decorated as Ida's.

Harbor peered around the soldiers. Usually, her father

came on the first launch boat, but there was no sign of him. Perhaps he was being cautious.

Peter slunk back toward the old shack at the end of the dock. He had studied soldiers for years, their uniforms and weapons and the battles they fought. He had pored over books in the library. Now, though, with this small battalion in front of him, he felt he could not look.

Frank stood by the shack. He put a hand on Peter's shoulder, and Peter jumped. "It takes some getting used to," Frank told him.

Peter could only nod.

"They mean well," he said. "Magic is tricky business, though. Once you get used to it, you realize the glittering, adventurous life you thought you were getting really isn't that different from your old life."

"This is entirely different than my life," Peter said.

Frank reached deep into his pocket and pulled out a hard candy. He handed it to Peter who took it wordlessly and slipped it into his mouth.

Harbor ran to the end of the dock and watched the boats coming in.

She did not see her father. Was he staying on the *Downeaster*? Perhaps she was meant to go with him, now that her curse had been broken. That would make sense. He was likely arranging things on board for her.

She turned to run back to the cottage to gather her things and saw her mother clasping Ida's hands. She pushed through the crowd to make her way back to them. "The Frost are nearly on our shores," Ida was saying. "He had to stay and fight. He sent me in his stead."

The crowd murmured like a single being. Harbor could feel the fear coming off them, sick and warm.

Queen Coralie put her hand on Ida's shoulder. "Come, let us speak in the hotel." She turned to Brigid. "Set these soldiers up by the cliff. Set a meal for them."

Brigid, with the scarcest of glances at Ida, turned and marched toward the low cliff at the far edge of the village where the plumrose tree grew. The Lapistyr soldiers followed her, their boots stomping in time.

Frank took off his hat and rubbed his hair. "Some of the other islands had soldiers on them," he said, more to himself than to Peter. "But never us. Never Dirigo."

Ida turned her attention to Harbor. Ida crouched in front of Harbor, who blinked back tears. Her father *always* came in her birthday month. She had been pricked and word had been sent. Yet her father hadn't come.

Ida took her helmet off and placed it on the ground beside her, a sign of respect. Ida pulled a small wooden box from her pocket. Harbor knew it was made from wood from Benspeir. Its top was engraved to look like gemstones and inlaid with green. "Your father bid me bring you this. It was especially made for you." Harbor pulled a pin and the top of the box popped open.

"Harbor, my sweet Harbor Rose," her father's voice cracked.

She snapped the box closed.

"It's a music box," Ida explained. "He had the toy maker capture his voice for you."

"That's so cool!" Peter said.

Harbor carefully opened the box again. "Harbor, my sweet Harbor Rose," came her father's voice again, slower this time. She'd recognize that voice anywhere: low and rich as autumn leaves. "My birthday wishes for you travel across the sea, though I cannot. Our world is not as I wish it were for you. I aim to fix that for you and for all The Lands of Lapistyr. But, back to those wishes. Here are the wishes I have for you this year. May you find the most wonderful treasures in The Place Where Things Wash Up. May Mary Templeton bake you a delicious cake. May the sun pinken your cheeks. May the winds blow you back to me. I love you, Harbor Rose. Happy birthday."

The voice stopped. Harbor closed the music box. She placed it in one of her pockets. "Thank you," she said to Ida.

Harbor knew it was a very nice gift. The box was beautiful. The toy maker recording her father's voice was a wonder. But the box was not her father, and he was what she truly wanted.

"I am sure your father will be pleased to hear that," Ida said. But she did not say when her father would hear the message or when Harbor might see him again. She simply left, chatting with the queen as she went.

"You're really a princess?" Peter asked.

Harbor nodded.

"And that's the queen?" he asked, pointing up the hill where her mother walked, the sun catching the red in her hair.

"Yes," Harbor said. "My mother. We must go."

Peter kicked at the dock.

"What's wrong?" Harbor asked.

"I'm not a prince or a king or anything," he said. "I don't know how to help. I don't know anything."

Peter's moods shifted like the winds, sudden and sharp. "You know about Kansas and la-crosse." The word tasted strange in her mouth. "Now you've been to the ocean more than once. You've seen far more of the world than I have. You've been to more than one of The Many Realms, and you understand a great deal about how they work."

Peter wouldn't look at her. Just kept digging his toe into the wood. "What was the thing about heroes?" he asked, a little hope edging his voice. "I remember you saying that before."

"It's the curse," she said. "When I was born, my mother's sisters all came to bless me at my christening. Opal Pearl, Sapphire, Ruby, and Amethyst. My parents didn't invite Micah. She had gone to The Somewhere Else, or so we were told, and no one had heard from her in years."

"And she came back all mad that she'd been overlooked and cursed you," Peter said.

"Exactly. How'd you know?"

"Everybody knows this story," he said. "You're pricked and you sleep a hundred years."

"No," Harbor said, shaking her head. "The prick was supposed to kill me. All of us, actually. But Amethyst fixed it. Mostly. I sleep and then the hero comes."

"Me?" he asked.

"Yes, you," she said. "It must be you. I was pricked, I slept, and then you washed up. That's why they sent you back last time. You were too young." She paused. "Do you think they knew? That time was different there?"

Harbor's thoughts were all a jumble: it was clear her parents and aunts knew things they weren't telling her, but there were also things they didn't know or didn't fully understand. Harbor didn't know which was which, and all of it made her angry.

Frank placed a hand on her shoulder. "I suppose you two ought to run along for now. All sorts of talking is going to have to happen again."

Harbor thought of the last time Peter had arrived, how they had spent the day exploring the island and all the wonder he had felt. Peter must have been thinking about it, too, for he turned to Frank and said, "Are there really giants on this island?"

"Not for many a year," Frank told him.

"That's what I figured," Peter said. Then he asked Harbor, "Do you think we might eat some of those peachy tomato things?"

"Plumrose fruit?" Harbor asked. "Fine, come this way."

She stomped away with Peter behind her. The box

thumped against her leg. A voice in a box was nothing like an actual father. A voice in a box couldn't hug you or answer your questions or tell you funny stories.

Peter struggled to keep up as she climbed toward the cliff. The plumrose tree was heavy with fruit. Harbor plucked two plumrose fruits and gave one to Peter.

"Sucks about your dad," Peter said.

"Pardon me?" Harbor asked.

"It just sucks," he said. "Not cool. A big letdown. I get it. My dad was supposed to come watch me play in this big lacrosse game. It was against our rivals. I was starting in goal. I played an amazing game. Like, truly. Twenty-one saves. My dad, he didn't show. And it wasn't even anything important like saving a whole realm or whatever."

Harbor wasn't sure if this soliloquy was meant to make her feel better. It didn't. She didn't know what lacrosse was, but if it was something you played at, it couldn't be very important. She crunched into her plumrose fruit. It was sour, not yet ripe. Of course.

Peter took a bite of his own fruit. After he swallowed, he said, "Anyway, I am sorry he flaked. Dads are kind of terrible sometimes."

Harbor's whole body burned. "My father is not terrible."

Peter held up his hands as if she might attack. "Okay, okay. Sorry."

"My father is as big and strong as the trees of Benspeir. He is a just and good king. He scoops me up, and he smells

128

like maple trees." She sniffled. Her father was all those things. But he had also chosen not to come see her. He had "flaked," as Peter had said. She didn't want to admit how much that hurt. "He is the king, and while my mother is away from Lapistyr, he must act as he sees fit to protect our people and our lands."

"Okay," Peter said again. "I was only trying to be nice."

Harbor knew this was true, but it didn't make her any less angry. She hated feeling angry. She hated the way it itched at her skin from her toes to her scalp. She especially hated it when she wasn't sure who she was angry at: her father for not showing, Peter for comparing his petty problems to hers, or herself for being selfish and small. Or maybe she was mad at her mother and aunts for once again going off and making decisions without her. Maybe she was angry at everyone and everything.

Peter finished his plumrose fruit. "These are amazing. I wonder if I could bring some back with me."

"We have to go," Harbor said.

"Go? Where?"

"To the hotel," she said. "We have to hear what's happening and how we can stop The Frost."

CHAPTER EIGHTEEN

Leo Murphy had years of practice looking down his nose disdainfully, and he put all those years to use when he stared at Harbor and Peter from the steps of the hotel.

"Hello!" Harbor said.

Leo's look grew even more disdainful. "I don't suppose you think you're going in there?" he asked, but it wasn't a question at all.

"We are," Harbor said.

"You aren't," Leo replied.

"We are," Harbor said again.

Perhaps it would have gone back and forth like that for hours, but Peter said, "That's okay."

Harbor snapped her head around. "It's not okay!"

"Take the boy's advice," Leo said. "At least he has some sense of propriety." Propriety was the thing Leo Murphy valued above all else. He did not really think Peter was demonstrating much of it, what with his cotton shirt not tucked into his short pants, all of them in galling colors including a shade of green not found in nature.

"I am the princess, and he is the hero. Our attendance is needed at this meeting."

"Your mother specifically declared you were not to attend."

Harbor scowled but knew there was no sense arguing. "Come on," Harbor said to Peter.

When they had made their way up the road a bit, Peter asked, "Where are we going now?"

"We're going to that meeting, of course," Harbor said.

"But your mother said we couldn't, and she's the queen."

"Well, she's wrong."

Peter stopped walking in the middle of the road. "I don't know," he said. "I don't want to get in trouble. I've never gotten in big, big trouble before, and trouble with a queen and her witchy sisters seems extra big."

"They aren't witchy," Harbor said. "And you're supposed to be a hero."

"I guess." Peter was realizing that thinking of oneself as being a hero and being heroic were two entirely different things.

"Good," Harbor said. "Let's go."

She led him up the road, then down a sandy path that deposited them behind the hotel. "I just want to listen," she whispered. "They never tell me anything."

They crept to the windows that looked onto the grand study. Bookshelves lined the walls filled with dusty tomes. Heavy, velvety furniture loomed around the room, but everyone stood: her four aunts, her mother, and Ida.

"So close?" Amethyst asked.

"That's what their messengers told us," Ida replied.

Peter elbowed Harbor. "Who are they talking about?"

"The Frost," she replied, but said no more. She wanted to hear what her mother and aunts were saying. She leaned her ear closer to the window.

Queen Coralie paced the room, looking small and fragile. "If they make it to Lapistyr, they may make it here as well."

"The king will make a brave stand," Ida said. She stood with her hands clasped behind her, her back ramrod straight. Harbor had always been impressed by the ornate uniforms, the shininess of the buttons, but now Ida's appearance made her uneasy.

"Bravery is not all that is required to win wars," Opal Pearl remarked.

"Our armies are strong," Ida said. "But the king recognizes defeat is a possibility or that a smaller group may splinter off to find the queen and princess. That is why I am here, and I will serve under your command, my queen."

"My command?" Coralie asked. "I have no military mind. None of us do!"

"We should flee," Amethyst said.

"And go where?" Opal Pearl asked.

"And what of the people here?" Ruby asked.

"We could bring them. All of them," Amethyst said. "We hid them once, we can hide them again. It's the only way to fulfill our promise to keep them safe."

"My husband would not run," Queen Coralie said.

"Your husband is not of Lapistyr," Sapphire said.

"And so we come to that again," Coralie replied.

The argument went back and forth, round and round. No one spoke of Harbor or Peter. It made no sense. He was the hero. If a battle was coming, they would need him. It was time to start talking about his role.

Peter sat back on the grass. He plucked out strands and ripped them in two. He had been called from another realm to save them, yet he was sitting around, playing like a *child*. "Ugh!" she groaned.

Inside, the voices stopped. Sapphire held up a finger.

"Now you've done it," Peter whispered.

Sapphire crossed the room, threw the window open, and grabbed both children. She dragged them into the room where they collapsed on top of each other on the floor. Harbor pushed Peter off and leapt to her feet. "It's not fair you leaving us out of the conversation!"

"There is no fairness when it comes to war," Opal Pearl told her.

Ruby helped Peter to his feet and gave his shoulders a little pat. "Right as rain," she said to him.

Harbor ran to Amethyst, "How can you suggest we flee? Will you have us abandon our home?"

"This is not your home," Amethyst said softly.

"It is part of my lands. I will defend it!"

"She speaks like her father," Opal Pearl said.

"Yes!" Harbor said. "I do. My father would never retreat before the enemy arrived, and neither shall I." She stood tall, mimicking Ida's stance.

Her mother put her hand under Harbor's chin and tilted Harbor's face up to her. "Daughter, you are brave, just like your father. Fierce and loyal. But leadership does not always mean fighting. Sometimes the way to win is by hiding the thing you love."

The words made something click in Harbor. "Like you hid me," she said. But it didn't work! The curse said war would come and come it had. "We cannot hide from it. It will find us again."

"Harbor," her mother said in a warning tone.

Harbor wasn't going to stop, though. "Don't you see? There's nowhere we can run. Unless we want to spend the rest of our days running, we must stay and fight. We must—"

Sapphire interrupted, "You are a child, and children have no place in this decision-making."

"But I do! I am the one who can call the hero. Here he is! We are ready to fight!"

For his part, Peter had been sinking slowly back into himself. He crossed his arms over his chest as if shielding himself.

"What say you, Peter?" Ruby asked gently.

"I—I'm not sure."

Harbor scowled while Ruby tut-tutted at Peter. "It is a very big thing to be asked to be a hero."

Harbor could not believe what she was hearing. Talk of running away. Letting the hero off the hook. Acting as though they weren't in imminent danger from a threat that would keep coming and coming and coming. "We're not asking! He *is* the hero. There's no asking involved!"

"Look at you, talking like you know the way of curses and blessings," Sapphire said, nearly laughing at how ridiculous it was.

Harbor held her ground. She was a child, true, but the adults weren't seeing things clearly. They were frightened. Their age made them cautious. Too cautious.

"Sapphire," Amethyst said. "Be kind."

"This is no time for kindness," Sapphire replied. Her hair splayed around her head as though the silver strands had been struck by lightning. The magnifying glass around her neck glinted. She was all light and anger.

Harbor was not afraid. "It's a time for heroes!" she exclaimed. "It's a time for Peter!"

Opal Pearl shook her head and said, "We don't know that," while Amethyst argued again that they should run, and Ruby fussed over Peter. The voices got louder and louder. The air in the room pulsed with anger and fear.

Peter clutched his arms more tightly around himself. "I'm not sure I'm ready, Harbor," Peter whispered to her. "If I just had a bit more time to prepare."

"You've had years!" Harbor yelled at him. His face turned bright red. He stared at his sneakers.

"Enough!" Sapphire cried. She fixed her gaze on Peter and murmured words too low to hear.

A trapdoor appeared beneath his feet and opened all at once. Peter dropped into it and was gone.

"Sapphire!" Queen Coralie cried. "Such a show of singular magic is dangerous!"

"So is that boy so long as he is here before his time."

Harbor scarcely heard them. "Peter!" she cried and dropped to the floor. Where once there had been a boy and then a trapdoor, there was now only wood.

CHAPTER NINETEEN

Harbor would never forgive Sapphire. She knew this in her heart of hearts and in the scowl she could not keep from her face. She was mad at Amethyst for wanting to run and her mother for not sticking up for the king and at Ruby for fussing so much over Peter and Opal Pearl for not stopping Sapphire. But, most of all, she was furious at Sapphire for not listening to her and for sending Peter away.

While Harbor stewed, work started on the island. Archie Murphy drew plans for a fort, and the villagers worked from sunup to sundown to build it. Harbor helped as best she could, pushing wheelbarrows full of stones to build the walls. But the queen and her aunts insisted she keep on with her lessons. Up in Opal Pearl's studio, she painted a watercolor of the sea.

"Flat," Opal Pearl told her. "Put some life in it."

"I don't want it to have life," Harbor responded. "I like it like this. Flat and calm."

Opal Pearl put down her sculpting knife. One of her long braids swung and brushed Harbor's shoulder, as gentle as the brush Harbor used. They looked out Opal Pearl's window, out to the ocean.

Harbor noted the rocks, the lighthouse, the birds that flew in the sky. Opal Pearl helped her to add each to her painting. She stood close, her body warm against Harbor's. As Harbor tried to add a golden light to the tip of her lighthouse, the paint mixed with the blue, turning into a green splotch. It looked like algae.

"Ugh!" Harbor cried. "Why are we even doing this? What does it matter if I can paint if I'm never at court? What does it matter if the invaders come? I'm not an ordinary princess— why do I have to do these princess things?"

"We continue about our business so we remember what we are fighting for," Opal Pearl explained. "We make art because art is creation and creation is essential in the path of destruction."

"Why do they come for us?"

"They have been sailing around the sea, claiming lands and people." Opal Pearl leaned back and looked at the ceiling where she hung her mobiles alongside drying herbs and pieces of objects salvaged from the ocean. "Lapistyr's lands are fertile and prosperous," she said. "We have been at peace for a long time. Your father is right to fear we are a target."

"We're only a target because of Micah's curse. She sent them to find us!"

"That is one way of looking at it," Opal Pearl said. She looked at a sculpture of a tree she had been making. It stood tall in the center of the studio, still unfinished. The stones along the trunk looked heavy and dull. With a crook of her finger, Opal Pearl made the tree start to spin. The buds of flowers bloomed and plumrose fruit grew. The fruit fell; the leaves blew away. Over and over through the cycle. "Wars are as old as time. If not them, perhaps it would have been some other enemy."

"Do you think we will be safe?" Harbor asked.

Opal Pearl didn't answer at first. She looked out over the sea. "Once men get their minds set to war, it can be hard to dissuade them. Harder to stop than the rolling tide."

"But the tide goes back out again," Harbor said.

Opal Pearl smiled. She held up her hand to stop the spinning tree. "Yes, dear, it does. And then rolls back in."

Harbor closed her eyes and leaned against her aunt. Opal Pearl looked toward the horizon and shuddered at what she saw there.

PART THREE

CHAPTER TWENTY

One day later, it was time to leave.

Opal Pearl saw the ships as she stared out at the sea with Harbor: little dots that Harbor mistook for birds.

Sapphire saw them clear as day through one of her telescopes.

Ruby saw them in her tea leaves.

Amethyst, sensitive as she was, felt the fear coming off her sisters. She pulled an atlas from a secret shelf and tried to trace the invaders' path across pages of maps.

Opal Pearl stashed her artwork and supplies in her cabinets. She placed a pot of ink, a brush, and three round stones into her satchel. When she left her studio, she locked the door behind her.

Sapphire extinguished the light in the lighthouse and sounded the horn five times in quick succession before pulling her dinghy in and lashing it to the lighthouse itself. Then she went about destroying her dock so the invaders could not come close.

Ruby slid bottles and jars into a stiff leather bag. She packed the fruits and vegetables she had canned, as many as she could. Scouts could go back for more, she decided. Or she could go herself, she thought, reminding herself that now was the time for bravery.

Amethyst made ready a stack of books, the most important ones, and bound them together with a leather strap. She placed them by the back door of the library so she could grab them at a moment's notice. Then she said her goodbyes to the books. It was not time for her to leave, not yet, but she wanted to make sure she had a chance to pay her respects to each of them. Books and libraries, she knew, were often the victims of war.

In the small cottage, Queen Coralie packed a suitcase while she ordered Harbor to do the same. "A bit of everything. We don't know how long we'll be gone."

They had expected to have more time, to move things out properly. Now they were leaving in a hurried fashion. Harbor tugged clothes from hooks in the closet. She tucked special trinkets into any spare space she could find: a small mirror, a piece of sea glass shaped like a heart, and the wooden girl Frank had carved for her.

Her mother burst into her room and tore the quilt from Harbor's bed. "Hurry!" she cried.

The last thing Harbor grabbed was Lucretia. She couldn't take both dolls, and Sweetwater was the larger of the two.

But perhaps a princess facing war, and a twelve-year-old princess at that, ought to be too old for dolls. She placed Lucretia back on the shelf. "You watch over the house like the hero Peter says you are."

She wished her father were here. As she had this thought, a more dangerous one followed: What if The Frost had already reached Lapistyr? What if her father were defeated?

"Harbor!" her mother called.

Harbor trotted down the steps two at a time. Her mother thrust her cloak at her, though it was too hot to wear it that day. Harbor tucked it under her arm, and they left the little cottage, the only home Harbor remembered.

"Where are we—"

"Shh!" her mother said.

Harbor frowned but said nothing more. Her bags were heavy, and her suitcase *thunked* against her legs. She squinted against the sun. Sweat gathered on her forehead, her back, her neck. She wanted to drop her cloak but worried she would need it for the cool evenings.

Her mother brought her around Opal's cottage to the trail behind that led to the woods. *The woods!* They were never meant to go there. "You said these woods were dangerous!" Harbor stopped short.

Her mother, after a moment's hesitation, said, "We must. Danger is always relative."

As they stepped past the first few trees, Ida emerged as if out of nowhere. She bowed her head, her long braid swinging forward. "Your Majesty," she said.

"Ida," her mother replied, in a clipped, formal tone Harbor didn't recognize. "What news?"

"The canopy is ready. Porters are on their way to guide you. I'm to the fort." She glanced at Harbor, then stepped closer to the queen. "Brigid is our scout. She will carry messages. Only she should leave the forest."

"I understand," the queen replied. Then she grasped Ida's hands, her queenly disposition dropped, and she was just Coralie. "Be well, Ida. Take good care and don't hazard any unnecessary risks."

Ida nodded and then dashed off with hardly a glance to Harbor.

"Mum, what is this? What's happening?" Harbor asked.

Her mother turned. They were nearly the same height now, but still her mother cupped her face in her hands and tilted it up to her. Tears welled in her mother's eyes. "Oh, Harbor," she said. "This is not at all as I had planned it. There are deeper legends for me to tell you, and little time. Our Small Island is under attack from The Frost—" She blinked the tears from her eyes. "Perhaps there will be a time of quiet when I can tell you all, but for now, you must know this: you are our hope. Our dreams rest with you." She touched Harbor's chest below the charms of her necklace: the globe of Lapistyr sand and the mysterious lens from Sapphire. "You must be safe, do you understand?"

Harbor nodded.

"You don't, child, you don't understand at all." Fear edged into her voice. She pulled Harbor close to her and spoke directly into her ear. "You must be safe, Harbor. No matter what else, *you* must be safe."

Harbor wasn't sure what her mother meant. Before she could ask another question, a group of low-ranking soldiers, recently arrived from Lapistyr, approached. They took the bags and belongings from Harbor and her mother. A boy not much older than Harbor herself took her cloak. His cheeks burned pink, and his uniform seemed a size or two too large. Harbor wanted to ask her mother why Lapistyr was employing soldiers as young as this one, but her mother was giving instructions to the lead soldier.

The boy soldier said, "Hurry on, miss. These woods are dark and dangerous."

Harbor trotted behind him. Perhaps he was not truly a soldier, but an apprentice of sorts, sent to aid the soldiers with their daily needs. Yes. That made much more sense.

The soldiers led them deeper and deeper into the forest. There were paths, but they were unmarked and hard to discern. Harbor tried to keep track, even stopping from time to time to stand up a rock on its edge or bend a skinny branch of a tree. Always she was urged to move faster, and after a while she realized she would never be able to find her way back out.

The soldiers led them on until they came to a small clearing. Sitting on a stump in the center was Ruby. Her cheeks glowed red, and her eyes were bright, but there was a sadness about them as well. "Welcome to my forest," she said. "I hope you will be at home here."

"Home?" Harbor asked. "But there's nothing here."

Ruby spread her arms wide and tilted her head back. "Ah, but there is. All you must do is look."

Harbor tilted her own head back. It took a moment for it all to come into focus, and then, all at once, it appeared.

There was a whole village in the canopy!

"Isn't it grand?" the boy soldier whispered to her. He was immediately hushed by an officer. But the boy was right: it was grand! Tiny cottages had been built on the strong branches of the old trees. They were connected by bridges that blended into the limbs of the trees. The tiny homes were nearly camouflaged by the foliage.

"But—"

"Over here, Harbor!"

Harbor spun her head and saw Brigid poking her head out of a window of one of the tree houses. A moment later, a ladder dropped. Harbor looked to her mother, who nodded. Harbor climbed the tree into the small house. There were two cots, a small table, and a shelf.

"Welcome to your castle, Your Highness," Brigid said with a laugh.

Harbor didn't know what came over her, but she launched herself at Brigid, wrapping her arms around her friend, and burst into tears.

"There now," Brigid said, stroking her hair. "I know this is a frightening time, but we're safe here. If those soldiers happen to bumble their way this far into the forest, we keep as quiet as mice and they won't find us."

Harbor nodded.

"But if somehow they do find us," Brigid said, "I brought this for you." She pulled back a curtain and revealed a bow and a quiver of arrows. The bow was carved of scarlet wood. Rosebuds were etched into the wood. The string was green. "A perfect bow for our Harbor Rose. Pray you never need to use it, but if you do, there you are." Then Brigid grinned. "Come on now," she called, already pushing open a small door and making her way out onto the bridge.

The rope bridge swung gently as they walked. Below, the soldiers bustled about, helping the villagers into their cottages. Mary Templeton directed the soldiers where to put her baking supplies while Leo Murphy decried the state of his boots. "So much mud along the path you brought us," he said. "So much mud." Tommy Murphy shook his head at Leo and told the young soldier he had done his job well.

On the outskirts of the clearing stood Frank. "Frank!" Harbor cried. "Frank, up here!"

Frank gave a wave but didn't move from his spot. He peered back into the woods.

"It's okay, Harbor," Brigid said. "People need some time to adjust. Come on, I have more to show you."

Brigid showed her how the ladders rose and fell to keep them safe. "Look, I've even had them put in some rope swings in case we need to get down in a hurry." She unlatched a rope from a branch. "Give it a go?"

"Where is everyone else?" she asked.

"The others will be coming. They are buttoning up the village. The soldiers will stay in the fort, and the rest of us will be here." As if reading confusion on Harbor's face, Brigid said, "It's safe this way."

"The fort was meant to keep us safe."

"It will. But just in case a couple of their lot make it onshore, we will be well hidden back here."

Harbor looked to Frank again. He crouched now, whittling a bit of wood, keeping his eyes trained toward the forest.

Harbor knew she was meant to feel safe in this space, but all she felt was dread.

CHAPTER TWENTY-ONE

They had been living in the forest for only a couple of days, but already there was a rhythm to the hours. Archie Murphy chopped wood for the small fires they used to cook their food. Mary Templeton kneaded dough while Mr. Broom gathered herbs. Harbor practiced with her new bow, aiming at the trees. The bow was of a much higher quality, but Harbor's aim seemed worse than ever.

Harbor, bored, offered to go in search of tabor root for Ruby. It was full of protein to help them stay healthy and strong, and Ruby worked it into a delicious stew. Harbor took her bow and quiver along with a basket.

"There's a chill coming," Ruby said, and she took the scarlet scarf from her own head and wrapped it around Harbor's, tying it tight beneath the chin. "There you are, my sweet, red as a blooming poppy. Stick to the paths. They are easy to follow, but tempting to leave."

"Yes, Ruby," Harbor said, but Ruby was already gone,

taking the herbs from Mr. Broom and begging the old man to sit and rest.

They had dug most of the roots close to the encampment, so Harbor had to venture deeper into the woods than she had ever gone. The paths were easy to see, just as Ruby had promised.

She spotted the green-and-purple shoots of the tabor root and squatted to begin digging. As she did, she saw, just beyond them, the most beautiful patch of flowers she had ever seen. She thought she knew everything that grew on the island, but these were something new. They grew taller than her and had, heavy on their stems, bright orange flowers that exploded like fireworks. Harbor left her basket in the patch of tabor root. Her steps took her away from the path. Ruby's warning was lost. The flowers were so lovely, so grand.

Standing in the center of the flowers, she reached up and touched one of the buds ever so gently. Petals rained around her, but the flower itself grew even bigger. "Oh," Harbor sighed.

"Lovely, aren't they?"

Harbor froze.

"These flowers are for you, Harbor Rose. Go ahead and pick them if you like."

Harbor spun around slowly. There was no one behind her. Then she looked up. A figure sat on a tree branch in a shimmering gray cloak. The woman stood and began walking along the branch. Harbor stepped back, her heart racing.

"It's quite all right," the woman said. "I won't fall. I have tremendous balance, you see. It's what I'm known for." She walked along the branch, and as she did so, it bent toward the ground until she could hop, neatly, onto the pine needles and dried leaves with hardly a sound. She dropped into shadows and Harbor could not see her face. A shape emerged beside her.

A wolf! It lifted its head, regarded Harbor, and yawned lazily.

All at once the words that Harbor's aunt had told her rushed back into her head. *Stick to the paths.* So, too, came all the stories of wild creatures that lived in the forest. She lowered her shaking hand.

"Everything on this island is for you, isn't that right?" the woman said. Harbor couldn't see her face, only her lips and tongue as she spoke. "Every flower, every creature. Why, even this wolf is for you."

"I—" Harbor began. "I'll scream if you come one step closer."

The woman cocked her head to the side. "If you are afraid of me, why not shoot me with one of your fine arrows?"

Harbor gripped her bow. "Perhaps I will."

"I don't think you will. I do not think you have ever shot at a single living thing, only the targets that little Brigid makes for you." She grinned. "And those you rarely hit. I don't have much to fear from you."

Harbor's whole body shook. The woman was right. Even

if she wished to shoot an arrow, it would never fly straight. "How do you know Brigid's name? How do you know mine?"

"I know everything about you, *my sweet*." She took a step out of the shadows, but her face was still hard to see. She smiled. "My, what a lovely red scarf. All the better for enemies to see you with, my dear."

Harbor pulled the scarf from her head. "Who are you? What do you want?"

"You should know who I am if this world had any sense. If your mother had any of hers left, perhaps we would not be in this situation at all. Your father, now, there is a man who was born without sense. For him, the only solution for a problem is to shoot it."

Harbor yanked an arrow from her quiver and struggled to nock it. "Why you—you can't say such things about the queen and king! I ought to shoot you where you stand!"

"So much more father than mother, then. Such a disappointment." The woman held up her hands. "Go on then. Though you might want to save your arrow for that."

Harbor turned and saw someone. Something? It was person-like, but not a person. The skin of the creature, whiter than white, glistened and sparkled and *moved*. "The Frost!" she cried and let her arrow go.

It flew crooked and only grazed the creature's arm. The creature looked at the smear of silver blood. For a moment, Harbor thought she saw fear or horror there. But then the creature smiled at her with silver teeth. Lightning quick, it lunged in her direction.

She took another arrow and let it fly. Another grazing shot. This time it hit the creature's leg. It limped on toward her.

"Hurry, hurry," the woman said. "What was it Brigid said about the heat of battle?"

Harbor took another arrow from her quiver. She pressed the nock into the string, listened for the click. She pulled back on the string. *Breathe*, came Brigid's voice in her head. Harbor did. A long inhale in, and then, with the exhale, she let go.

The arrow flew straight and true. It whistled through the air. The creature stopped. It pushed its chest forward like a target. The arrow hit the creature right in its heart.

The creature fell to the ground with a dull thud.

"Go see," the woman said. "Go see what you have killed."

Harbor did not want to see but felt compelled. She stepped toward the body. As she did, color seeped into the skin. It was not a creature at all. It was human. A girl not much older than herself with brown eyes and freckles and hair the color of maple leaves in late fall. She blinked her eyes. "Thank you," she whispered to Harbor.

Then she was gone.

CHAPTER TWENTY-TWO

What—" Harbor cried, but she wasn't sure how to finish her questions. *What was that? What happened to her? What did I do? What did you do?* The questions tumbled around in her head, none of them able to get out. She could only stare at the spot on the ground where the girl had once been. Now there was only grass and old, dead leaves completely frozen over.

"I'm sure this is all very confusing," the woman said. Her cloak caught the light and shimmered. "That was one of The Frost."

"That was a *girl!*" Harbor yelled. "A person. A child. Now she's just . . . gone."

"For a moment she was a girl again. Thanks to you."

"I killed her! I killed a girl." Harbor's knees felt weak. She put her hand out and leaned against the tree.

The wolf, who had not been very interested in the occurrences of the past few minutes, whined softly.

"You killed The Frost, and The Frost took her with it," the woman said. "It's a subtle distinction to be sure, but I wouldn't beat myself up too much about it if I were you. Now, lollygagging and looking at flowers while The Frost attack your seemingly safe encampment, that's something to beat yourself up about."

"What do you mean?" Harbor asked. She felt ill. Her vision was clouded. The words the woman spoke came into her head, but she could make no sense of them.

"The Frost," the woman said and pointed at the ground. "This was a scout. One of many. They will surely find your encampment at any moment. Then all you love will be overcome."

"By The Frost soldiers?" Harbor said slowly. "By the children?"

"Some of them were children once. Some grown-ups. Even a few dogs, I'm told."

"Dogs?"

"But none of them are what they once were, and they won't be again until you let them free."

"I can free them?" Harbor asked. "How?"

"By killing them. Then they will be free. And then they will be dead. But The Frost will grow weaker with each death, and for that I am sure they will thank you."

"But," Harbor began. "But that can't be it. That can't be the only way."

The woman only shrugged.

"Wait," Harbor said. "I know you."

"Indeed you do," the woman said.

"You were there," Harbor said. "The morning I was pricked. You were there. Did you put that pin there? Who are you?"

"So many questions," the woman said.

Harbor was furious and confused and ready to scream because of all the emotions swirling around in her. But before she could scream, someone else did—far off in the woods, high and loud.

Harbor spun. Smoke rose from the forest. When she turned back to face the woman, the woman was gone.

Harbor had no choice but to run. She sprinted as fast as she could toward the scream and the smoke.

❧❧❧

When she arrived at the camp, Harbor spied Frost soldiers through heavy smoke. They climbed the ladders. They climbed the trees.

Brigid fought off a soldier with her sword. Brigid thrust forward. "No!" Harbor cried. The smoke stung her throat.

The soldier fell. Brigid ran to Harbor. "Harbor! You're safe! We must go. Ida told me I must find you and keep you safe. I've been looking all over and—"

A Frost soldier leapt at them. Brigid swung her sword again. Harbor reached out her hand to stop her. The sword grazed the soldier, and it jumped back, silver blood oozing.

"Don't!" Harbor cried.

"This is war," Brigid said, her breath coming in huffs. She shook off Harbor and lunged at the soldier. She plunged her sword into the soldier's chest. The soldier fell backward, the whiteness of The Frost slipping off as he fell.

Brigid didn't see. She grabbed Harbor and tugged her toward the edge of the forest. "We must go."

"No!" Harbor said. "They aren't soldiers. They are prisoners. They are—"

"I care not who or what they are, Harbor. They are trying to kill us, and I am charged with keeping you safe. Now let's go."

Through the smoke, Harbor saw her mother. She had to get to her and tell her what she had learned. She shook off Brigid's arm and ran. "Mother!"

Her mother turned. "Harbor, run! Go!"

The yelling caught the attention of The Frost. They turned in two directions, splitting as if performing a dance. Half went toward Harbor, the other half to her mother. Brigid pushed Harbor out of the way. She swung her sword.

Harbor fell. Her eyes watered from the smoke.

Boots stomped around her. White boots of The Frost. Soft leather of her soldiers. Work boots of the villagers. They shook her body and made her teeth clack together.

She had to get away, get out, tell someone. Tell her mother. Tell Sapphire. Tell them what these soldiers really were.

She crawled below the smoke away from the boots.

The soldiers came and came and came. They were

possessed, she knew. The woman had said there was no way to stop them but—

Crash! A boot fell right beside her. She rolled out of its way, but hands grabbed her. They pulled her. Through the smoke, a familiar scent. "Frank!"

"Stay with me," he said.

With Harbor in his arms, he ran away from the fight in the encampment.

"Wait!" she cried. "Go back!"

"I can't save 'em all, Harbor girl."

"But the soldiers, they aren't what we think, they—"

Frank stumbled. The two fell in a twist of limbs. He grunted. She cried.

"Go," he whispered in her ear, urgent as spring rain. He pushed her.

Bootsteps clomped closer.

She crawled as fast as she could toward the bush. She pushed through it and found a safe den behind it. Her breath came hard and ragged. She had to go, had to—

Hands came for Frank. Now he was the one being picked up. Two soldiers hoisted him to his feet.

Harbor put her hand over her mouth. She bit her fingers. A scream fought to get out.

Frank. They had Frank. He could have gotten away if it wasn't for her. If she had run. If he hadn't been carrying her. If—

He was already changing. The color drained out of his

face. His lips curled into a sneer. His eyes flashed silver. He was her Frank. He was not at all her Frank.

She cried his name. "Frank!"

He turned, but he did not recognize her. His eyes were not his own anymore. Still sneering, he moved toward her. Slow and deliberate.

A hand fell on her shoulder. Tight.

Harbor snapped her head around. Sapphire. Her cloak was torn and muddy. She pulled Harbor, hard, into a thicket of trees and underbrush.

"They took Frank," Harbor cried.

"Hush!"

"They changed him!"

"You must go," Sapphire said.

"Don't hurt him," Harbor said. "Promise me you won't hurt him or any of them."

"I will do what I must," Sapphire said. Her glasses in her hair were cracked. The lens around her neck had smoked over.

"They are still there. Still inside."

Sapphire pressed something into her hand: a velvet pouch. "Take this. Go. The time has come to call our hero."

Harbor looked past Sapphire to the mass of white, glittering bodies. People who were her friends but not the people she had known.

She ran.

CHAPTER TWENTY-THREE

Go.

Sapphire's word echoed in Harbor's head. But go where? Did a single safe space on the island remain?

Harbor crawled through the woods on hands and knees. Sticks scraped her skin. Her fingers sunk into muddy spots. A snake slithered by her. She crawled on. Away from the noise. Away from the yells.

She rose up and broke out of the woods near the cliffs where she and Brigid had practiced their archery. Down the hill she could see what was left of her little village. White smoke drifted from the rubble.

Harbor swayed on her feet.

The hotel, Mr. Coffin's store, Frank's skinny little blue house—all gone. These things she had taken for granted, these places she had assumed would always be there, were gone.

"No!" she cried, then slapped her hand over her own mouth.

She retreated into the woods. With her knees to her chest and her mouth in her knees, she cried. She tried to keep as quiet as she could, but all that she loved was gone. Destroyed as if it meant nothing. To The Frost, it *was* nothing. Just something to be consumed. Something to—

A wail stuck in her throat.

The girl soldier. *Thank you*, she had said. Her dying words. Harbor had freed her from whatever spell The Frost had placed on her. Now The Frost were casting that spell on her friends and family.

Harbor crept toward the edge of the forest. She had to look.

White shapes moved over the walls of the fort and around the grounds. All was white and silver. All but the old plumrose tree that maintained its bright colors. She saw no familiar shapes: not Ida's graceful posture or Brigid swinging a sword or Mr. Coffin searching. Maybe that was a good thing. Maybe they had escaped.

She knew that wasn't true.

The sun was still high in the sky. It was only midafternoon, though it felt as if years had passed. She was not the same child who had gone searching for tabor root that morning, of that much, she was certain. Though who she was now was of little use to her. She was not brave like her father. She was not crafty like Frank. She did not have the magic of the Lapistyr women. Oh, what she would give for just a little of that magic!

She reached into her apron pocket and took out the music box from her father. She had carried it with her everywhere. She had gotten used to the way it *thunked* against her leg.

Carefully, she opened it.

"Harbor, my sweet Harbor Rose."

When she heard her father's voice, she could hold back her tears no longer. She sobbed so hard her body shook.

"May you find the most wonderful treasures in The Place Where Things Wash Up. May Mary Templeton bake you a delicious cake."

These wishes seemed so small. Tinny promises that held no weight in the real world.

"May the sun pinken your cheeks. May the winds blow you back to me."

Back. Back to her father. Oh, how lovely that would be. She'd curl up in his arms, place her head on his chest, and just breathe. He would stroke her hair and wonder at how much she had grown. She would tell him all the tales she had been storing up. It would be easy and lovely and safe.

But he was not here. He was not coming.

She wiped her nose and took a deep breath. Her father was not coming. Safety was not coming. She had to handle this herself.

She opened the pouch that Sapphire had given her. The

pin fell into her hand. The unicorn glinted menacingly in what was left of the sun.

She knew what she must do. Her father was not coming, and she could not call him, but there was someone she could call. Someone she must call. The thought of it frightened her to the bone. Once she pricked herself, she would sleep. Alone, no one to protect her, asleep—the thought made her tremble.

It wasn't a choice, though. It was her curse, her blessing, her duty. She had to call the hero. He would be older now—an adult ready to fight. He said he needed more time to prepare, and he'd had that time. He would arrive, and he would save them all. All she had to do was be brave enough to sleep.

Taking a path that led her behind Opal Pearl's house, she made her way to The Place Where Things Wash Up. In the little cove, she couldn't smell the smoke. Couldn't hear the yells of the soldiers as they moved around the fort. She breathed in. She smelled the salt in the air and felt it on her skin. She watched the waves go in and out.

The sea had always been there for her. It could be angry and stormy or calm and glittering, but it was always the sea. This was her home. These were her people.

She had to save them.

The old little boat, turned over so its bottom faced the sky, was the safest place for her to hide. It was tilted enough for her to crawl underneath it. She pushed herself all the way back where the sun barely reached. She wound herself into a tight coil with her bow beside her. Before she lost her nerve, she pressed the end of the pin into her finger.

A single drop of blood emerged.

Harbor fell asleep.

CHAPTER TWENTY-FOUR

Is that her?"

"Yes, that's her. She must still be sleeping."

"I thought you said she was a princess. She doesn't look like a princess."

Harbor blinked open her eyes. Two faces peered at her. The sun rose behind them. Peter. One of them was Peter. His curls were longer and spread around his head like a lion's mane. A bruise bloomed around his right eye.

"Peter?" she murmured.

"In the flesh," he replied. A grin spread over his face.

The girl next to him was small with locks of blonde hair that stretched down her back and stuck to her face. She shivered.

Peter turned to the girl. "I told you it was real. A whole other world through that door and a princess and curse. This is her! This is that place!" His smile grew even wider.

Sleep still clung to Harbor. Peter was here. She had called him. She had called him, and he had come. She had called him because—

"Peter!" Harbor cried. She scrambled out from under the boat and tried to stand. Peter caught her by the elbow to steady her. She shook him off. "We must go! We must hide!" They would go back to the woods, she decided. They would see if anyone had survived the attack and then make their plan.

She tugged him toward the path.

"What's that sound?" he asked.

Harbor's stomach dropped. Footsteps. The sound was an army marching toward them. They could not escape by land.

"Help me turn this over," she told him and started pushing on the boat. Peter crouched beside her, and together they flipped it over. "Come on, come on," Harbor urged. The little girl stared back at her with wide eyes. Why had Peter brought her? "Get in the boat," Harbor told the girl. Wordlessly the girl crawled in.

"What is happening?" Peter demanded.

The Frost coming over the crest was all the answer he needed. He started pushing the small boat toward the water. Harbor threw her bow and her quiver of arrows into the boat then pushed, too. The footsteps kept marching, a white wall racing toward them like a wave.

"Go, go, go!" Peter yelled.

"I'm going!"

The boat was fixed in the sand as if it were anchored. With a mighty grunt, Harbor pushed again.

The girl in the boat started crying.

Harbor thought of what Frank had taught her: never panic on a boat. That's when you make dangerous choices. Harbor ran to the bow. It was dug into the sand.

"Move to the stern!" she cried to the girl.

The girl did not move.

"Move to the back. The back of the boat."

Though the girl was small, her weight was enough to lift the bow ever so slightly. Harbor grabbed the tow line and pulled. Peter pushed.

The Frost got closer. Harbor did her best to ignore them. *Don't panic, don't panic, don't panic.*

Frank's voice took over for the voice in her head. *There's our girl. Steady on. Let the boat tell you how it wants to go.*

"Push!" she yelled to Peter as her feet touched water. "We're almost there!"

An arrow splashed into the surf.

Peter's face was red with exertion. He gave one last push. The boat floated.

"Get in, get in," Harbor said.

Peter clumsily climbed in, and Harbor dragged the boat out farther before jumping in herself. The Frost were still making their way to the cove. The narrow path slowed them down, but not by much.

Harbor yanked the oars from where they'd been stored,

prayed they were still solid. She dropped them into their locks and began to row.

She threw her whole body into it. She did not think about Frank and where he really was. She did not think about her mother and The Frost soldiers invading the encampment. She did not think about this little girl who sniffled at her feet. She most assuredly did not think about the woman in the woods or her wolf. Harbor thought about the strokes of her oars. She thought about the ache in her arms, the burn on her hands. She thought about moving. About escaping. About going.

She rowed and rowed and rowed. Sweat dropped from her face. It ran down her back. She rowed. A blister formed on her palm. She rowed. The blister popped. She rowed.

"Harbor? Harbor, I think we lost them." Peter's voice was soft, but it broke through her shell. "What happened here?" he asked.

That was when Harbor started to cry.

≈≈≈≈

Peter took the oars while Harbor told the story. She told them about The Frost and how her arrow seemed to have broken some sort of spell over the soldier.

"Like zombies," Peter said. "Or maybe more like vampires."

Harbor didn't know what he was talking about.

"Oh, or like mind control. Or like the Borg. They become

part of a collective, and killing them sets them free. I mean, for a minute."

The little girl sat still on the bottom of the boat. Her feet were in a small puddle of seawater. "Where are we?"

Peter took another stroke with the oars. "I told you. We're in another realm. This is Harbor; she's the princess. Harbor, this is Anna. My sister."

Harbor remembered he'd said his sister was six. This girl looked about seven or eight. "How long has it been?" she asked.

"Just about two years," Peter said. "I turned fourteen last week."

"I was hoping you'd be an adult by now."

The sun was starting to lower, and a wind was picking up. The smoke still drifted over the island, but it was lessening. They kept the shore in sight. Peter instinctively knew that they should not drift too far out to sea. They would have to come in sooner or later. Harbor wasn't sure where they could land. The back half of the island was nothing but trees and cliffs.

"What happened to your face?" Harbor asked.

Peter winced. "Cam. But he looks worse than I do."

There was a grittiness to his voice, an anger that hadn't been there before.

He'd been younger than her before, but now he was two years older. Fourteen was still a child but was closer to being an adult. Closer to being the age of a hero.

Her father, with his broad shoulders and thick beard, would eclipse Peter. But her father wasn't here. Peter was. Not an adult, to be sure, but maybe he was strong enough.

"I called you because we need you," Harbor told him. "Have you been preparing?" she asked. "Like you promised?"

"I—well, I've been playing a lot of D&D. Dungeons & Dragons. It's a game. You probably don't have it here. It's like a strategy role-playing game. I thought it would help me know what to do."

"A game? Lapistyr is in peril and you've been playing a game?" Harbor's voice echoed out over the sea.

"Yeah, well, there's not a whole lot of hero training academies in our realm. Sorry," he shot back, not sounding sorry at all.

Anna lifted her head. "If you're the princess and he's the hero, then we must be here to rescue you. Once we rescue you, then we can go home. That's the way this works."

"I suppose so," Harbor said. "The trouble with curses and blessings is that they are never quite clear. But my aunts can definitely send you home."

"Your aunts who have been captured?" Peter asked, his voice still icy. "Perfect."

"Well, I think they have been. I didn't see it for myself." Harbor didn't have much hope, but she didn't want to take away from what the others had.

"And you want me to rescue them?" Peter asked. His voice wavered slightly.

"Yes," she said.

Anna looked at the smoke that hung in the air. "You said it was magical here," she said to Peter. "This isn't like I imagined it at all."

Peter's rowing slowed. "It is magical here. You'll see. Once we get rid of the bad guys, we'll have some time to look around. I promise. Harbor's aunts really are magical and the ocean—you don't remember from our trip. That ocean was pretty. This one is—"

"Terrifying," Anna said.

"Beautiful," Peter said.

Harbor knew the ocean was both.

Peter re-gripped the oars and started pulling harder. As he did, all the hope and enthusiasm he'd shown his sister disappeared. He set his jaw tight as a trap. Anger radiated off him. Harbor burned it right back at him. He'd known they were going to call him back. He'd had years to prepare. He hadn't even learned to use a weapon!

They rowed in stony silence.

Finally, Peter sighed. "I guess I never really believed that was real," he said. "That I was a hero somewhere else."

Anna said, "I did."

Harbor held out her finger where the drop of blood still clung. "Every time I prick my finger, I fall asleep and you come."

"Did he kiss you?" Anna asked. "He didn't kiss you this time, but you woke up anyway."

Harbor felt her cheeks burn. "Why in heaven's name would he kiss me?"

"That's the story," she said. "The princess pricks her finger on a spinning wheel and falls asleep for a hundred years, and then a prince comes and kisses her, and she wakes up and they get married and live happily ever after."

"Anna likes those kinds of fairy-tale stories with Prince Charmings and balls and kisses and all that stuff."

"Oh," Harbor said. "Well, I think this was a different kind of curse entirely. I'm quite glad it didn't involve kissing."

"Gee, thanks," Peter said.

"Not that it would be terrible to kiss you," Harbor said. "I just don't think I would like anyone to kiss me while I was sleeping, without asking. Except my mother and my father. I like when they come and kiss me as I sleep. It wakes me a bit, but I don't mind at all." She sighed. The afternoon light was beautiful, golden, and pure. It would be so nice to forget for a moment all that was going on. It would be so lovely to be in this boat with her parents, fingers trailing in the water, laughing at jokes. Instead, she was with this boy who was not ready to fight and a little girl who was more hindrance than help.

Peter glanced at the sky. "How much farther is it?"

"I'm not entirely sure," Harbor said. Harbor had never ventured to the back side of the island and wasn't certain how large it was. Her plan was to row them around the island to the place with the rocks and the tidepools. From there, they could go up the hill and then skirt the forest, under-cover, to get back to the treetop retreat. She had to hold out hope that at least some people had survived the attack. At the very least, perhaps she could find or leave a message there.

Above them, birds called to one another. Waspgulls! How strange to see them so far from the plumrose tree.

"We're nearly around the east side, I should say. It's an oval shape. We'll come around the northern side, then back down the west a bit."

"So still a long way," he said.

Harbor nodded. "I'm afraid there's nothing on the back of the island. Only trees and more trees. Even if we could get up the cliffs," she said, pointing toward the wall of rock beside them, "we'd surely get lost in the forest."

But then, they rounded an outcropping of rock. Harbor gasped. She couldn't quite believe what she was seeing: a dock jutted out into the water with gulls standing on its pil-ings. Beyond the dock stood a whole village.

PART FOUR

CHAPTER TWENTY-FIVE

I don't know what this place is," Harbor said.

She leapt from the boat and tied it to the cleat. Grabbing her bow and arrows, she ran up the dock. Her head spun. There was nothing on the other side of the island. That was what everyone had always said. Yet here it was: a whole village.

The village was like her own, but smaller. Ghostly. There was a small shack at the edge of the dock with an open window. Its gray shingles were weathered, and some had fallen to the ground. Inside was an old sign advertising fresh bait.

Had they all just assumed the other side of the island was empty? Had no one explored? What Harbor was seeing and what she knew were crashing against each other, and she couldn't make any sense of it.

Harbor kept running. At first, she had thought this village was a mirror of her own, but as she got closer, she noticed the differences. Up on the main street was a string of shops, their windows coated over with dust and salt. One had a pole hanging outside with a blue-and-red swirl encased in glass. Another had a sign in the window: *Rationing means a fair share for us all!*

Harbor turned right and walked up the lane. The village wasn't as large as hers. The cluster of buildings opposite the harbor thinned out almost at once. A house overgrown with weeds looked ready to topple over. Behind it was a garden, just as overgrown.

"Tomatoes!" Peter cried. He pushed his way through the weeds. Anna was right behind him. He tossed her a tomato bigger than her fists, and she bit into it like an apple.

Juice dripped down her chin. "It's delicious!"

"What were those fruits you gave me?" Peter asked. "The tomato-plums?"

"Plumrose fruit," Harbor said.

"Right. Any of those trees around?"

"Only on the other side of the island," Harbor said. At least that was what she thought. This whole village wasn't supposed to be here. Maybe there was an orchard worth of plumrose trees.

"You want one?"

"I'm not hungry," Harbor said.

"I am!" Peter exclaimed. He noticed some sweet peppers growing and grabbed some of those, too. "It's been like hours or days or years—who knows? It feels like forever since breakfast; that's all I can tell you."

Harbor realized it had been hours since she had eaten, too. Hours that felt like days or weeks or years, but seeing the tomato juice dripping from their lips like blood turned her stomach. "We should keep looking," she said, though she wasn't sure what they should be looking for.

Peter and Anna followed Harbor from the garden back to the road.

"It's a ghost town," Anna said.

"There's no such thing as ghosts," Harbor replied. But she knew that ghosts weren't just spirits. They were feelings. This place thrummed with emotion and memory.

They came to a small white church with a red door that was dusty but still bright. The door stuck a little at first, but then gave way. Stale air and old incense greeted their noses. It was a simple church with a row of pews and small alter at the front. A table inside the door held an empty vase and a small stack of hymn books.

"It's like they just got up and left," Peter said. "But not in a rush. Everything is neat and organized. The people are just . . . gone."

Harbor backed out of the church, and they kept walking up the road. A small, brick building with a white door was at the end of the lane. Next to the door was a plaque that read, *Dirigo Island School*.

Harbor's heartbeat quickened. *Dirigo*. She knew that name.

They went into the one-room schoolhouse. Desks were lined up inside. Twelve of them plus a larger one for the teacher.

Twelve desks. Twelve desks for twelve children. But there were no other children on Small Island.

Harbor felt dizzy.

"Look," Anna said. "There's math on the chalkboard."

The numbers were written in a childish hand. The columns lined up and added together. One of the sums was done incorrectly.

Children.

The word rang in Harbor's brain. "This isn't right. Let's go, let's—" Her hands were shaking.

Peter touched her arm. "Are you okay?"

"I'm fine, I just—none of this makes any sense."

"Look at the date," Anna said.

Peter and Harbor noticed it at the same time. Written in neat script was *March 12, 1944*.

"That's impossible," Peter whispered.

Harbor was already running out the door.

ᖇᖇᖇᖇ

Children and schools and numbers on chalkboards—none of this was supposed to exist on Small Island. All her life she had been told that the forest—the dangerous forest—went all the way to the far side of the island. There was nothing there.

Harbor stood in the fading sun in this new village and breathed deep. The air smelled the same. The sea sounded the same.

She remembered her father coming once. She had said to him, "Let's sail around the island. Let's see how big it really is."

"An adventure is what you seek?" he asked. "Exploration?"

She had nodded eagerly and climbed the trunk of his body. They were nearly to the dock when Opal Pearl stopped them. She told them the currents were rough on the other side of the island. She told them that it was too risky for Harbor to go. They had settled for climbing the rocks. Harbor hadn't thought much of it then. She'd just been happy to spend time with her father. Now, though, she saw it for what it was: a lie.

"Well, my mind is blown," Peter said from behind her. "Like spaghetti in a blender."

Harbor wished he would stop talking so she could think.

"It doesn't make sense. Do you have dates here?" he asked. "You must have dates. But it probably isn't the same calendar. So, maybe that date didn't mean anything to you, but for me, for us, that was a long, long time ago. Like ancient history, practically."

Harbor straightened. Her brain was a scramble trying to make sense of everything. She looked down the street, past the barber shop. A name on a sign jumped out at her: *Coffin.*

"It can't be," she whispered and started walking. Peter and Anna followed. At the door, Harbor hesitated, but Peter opened the door and stepped inside with Anna right behind him. After a moment, Harbor followed. All the shelves were dusty and empty. Abandoned cobwebs hung in the windows like lace curtains. Stools were fixed into the floor in a line by the counter.

"It's like The Soda Fountain back home," Anna said.

Harbor looked to Peter to explain.

"The Soda Fountain. It's like this retro place. You can get ice cream and sodas and stuff. They wear silly hats."

"It's our favorite place because it's so old-fashioned. It's like playing make-believe," Anna explained.

"All this," he said. "It's like home—like our world or realm or whatever. But not like now—like old."

Harbor held her hands out to indicate the decay. "This is old, too. It's like no one has been here in years."

"No, I mean, like really old. Like in my grandparents' time. Maybe even before."

Harbor moved closer to the counter toward a big contraption with buttons and a drawer.

"Like that. That's an old cash register." Peter pushed a couple of buttons, and the drawer shot out. *Clang!* They all jumped.

The drawer was divided into different sections, each empty. Except—peering out from under the dust was the torn edge of paper. Harbor slipped it out and blew off the dust that fell like snow. It was a picture in black and white. Harbor squinted. The man in the picture looked just like Mr. Coffin. He had his arm around a woman who wore a simple gingham dress. She gave him the biggest smile.

"This place is creepy," Anna said.

"It's like World War Two times," Peter said. "That sign about rations. They had to do things like that back then. There wasn't enough stuff like sugar, so they limited how much people got. They had to use coupons . . ." Peter's voice drifted off. "Sorry, I watch a lot of history videos on You-Tube. Anyway, that's what all this reminds me of. Like a town from that era was frozen in time."

"But that's your realm," Harbor said. "Not mine."

"Fair point," Peter said.

Anna stayed close to Peter as he moved through the store. Harbor looked at the picture of Mr. Coffin again. Who was the woman? Mr. Coffin had no wife, no sisters. She couldn't deny, though, that it was him. Nor could she deny how much this shop felt like his. Even the lingering scent reminded her of his pipe smoke.

"Um, Harbor," Peter said. "You should see this." They were in the back of the store in a small office. Peter held up a sheath of gray papers. "It's a newspaper. From Portland, Maine. Do you have a Portland, Maine?"

Harbor shook her head.

Peter spread the paper out on the desk. "Yeah, see, I learned about this. The military was worried that an attack would come from Europe, so they built all these forts and stations on the islands off the coast of Maine. And German

U-boats came that far. They sunk a navy ship." Peter read more. "This is so cool. It's like the actual article from the actual time."

"What's it doing here?" Harbor asked.

Peter didn't have an answer for that. The questions were mounting up for Harbor, and she knew that no one could answer them, at least not anyone she could reach.

Her eye was caught by a story below the fold:

LINCOLN WRECKS.
MIRACLE BABY LONE SURVIVOR

Two photos went with the story. One showed the ferry wreckage: broken bits of wood floating on placid water. The other was of a fat baby wrapped in a blanket and sitting in a basket.

Three days after the wreck of the ferry boat *Lincoln*, a baby washed ashore on the southern side of the island. She was found by Richard Coffin at his usual beach-combing spot. The widower Mr. Coffin brought the child back to Dirigo Center. She is currently being cared for by Dr. Marlowe and his wife.

All at once, Harbor felt struck. She knew this baby. This basket. This boat. Yet she knew none of it. Her head spun. She ran her finger over the picture of the baby and felt her throat tighten as tears welled in her eyes.

"Harbor?" Peter asked.

Harbor kept reading.

It is believed the child was on the ferry, though that has not yet been confirmed. Not knowing her given name, residents have begun referring to her as the Sweet Harbor girl, named for the inlet where she washed ashore. Anyone with any knowledge of the child should contact their local police precinct.

"Are you okay?" Peter asked.

"Mr. Coffin found a baby," Harbor said. "You aren't the first person to wash up here."

"Huh, you think they came from our realm, too?"

"I think that baby is me," Harbor said. *Sweet Harbor girl.* That was what Frank had called her all her life. Some of the others, too. Could it be a coincidence?

"But this newspaper and stuff, this is from our realm."

"The Somewhere Else," Harbor said.

"Is that what you call it? I call it the real world, and you live in the magical world, but whatever. We can work on it. Anyway, it's like somehow this place—it's in your world, but also in my world."

"Amethyst told me there were thin spots. Maybe this is one of them."

Peter patted his pockets. He pulled something small and rectangular out of one. The thing seemed to be made of metal and glass.

"Maybe you're a changeling princess," Anna said. "Maybe fairies sent you."

"I think this means I'm not a princess at all," Harbor said. The words felt like a pit in her stomach, but they also felt true. It would explain so much: why she had to take those endless princess lessons, why she had no magic.

Peter poked and squeezed at the object.

"What is that?" Harbor asked.

"My phone," Peter said. He gave it a shake. "I thought maybe if we were in some in-between place, I might have service."

"A phone?"

"Yeah, a cell phone. You can call, like, over the air? Anyway, it won't work. It got wet. Totally dead."

Harbor wondered about a phone that could call across the realms.

"Oh!" Anna exclaimed. "Maybe you are a hidden princess. Like *Anastasia*."

"Enough with *Anastasia*!" Peter exclaimed.

"What's *Anastasia*?"

"It's her favorite movie. She likes it because the girl has the same name as her."

"It's a true story!" Anna exclaimed. "She was a Russian princess, and her family was imprisoned and she disappeared and some people think she was just living a normal life with some new name and story."

The story sounded familiar to Harbor. Perhaps Amethyst

had told it to her. She couldn't concentrate enough to try to remember. Her brain was still cycling.

"This is nothing like what Harbor is talking about. There was a shipwreck. She was on it. She washed ashore, and somehow she ended up in the hands of the king and queen."

Anna went on, "But what if she was a princess and her kingdom was under attack and so they sent her out in a little boat and they thought a common family would find her and raise her in safety, but instead she was found by a royal family and—"

"Enough," Peter said. He nodded toward Harbor, who was silently crying.

"Oh," Anna said. "I'm sorry. I was just thinking."

Thinking.

Somehow she ended up in the hands of the king and queen.

Harbor was pretty sure she knew what the *somehow* was.

CHAPTER TWENTY-SIX

Harbor's feet pounded the dry, dirt road as she thought of all the things she was not. Not a princess. Not magical. Not born in Lapistyr. Everything she had known about herself was untrue except for one thing: she was cursed.

Curses were funny. That was what everyone said. Not funny like they would make you laugh, but strange. You could never quite be certain of their meaning. Harbor had always known she was cursed but had never known quite how badly fate had chosen to harm her.

The ocean stretched out in front of her. What else didn't she know about? What other lies had she been fed? She had gone through life thinking the people who loved her most of all were telling the truth, and now she was faced with knowing her parents, her aunts, and her friends had all lied to her every single day of her life. Anger was too small a word to describe what she was feeling.

As she reached the dock, she sped up. She threw a wild scream into the air. She dove. The cold water pulled her close. The ocean still loved her. It twined its frigid fingers through her hair and around her toes. It squeezed tight around her lungs. Deeper and deeper and deeper, she swum. If she could just keep swimming down, just keep paddling farther out to sea, perhaps she could find where she was truly meant to be.

But she could not stay underwater forever. Her lungs began to ache. She pushed to the surface and gasped for air.

Peter stood at the end of the dock. "Did that help?" he asked.

"A little." She swam back to the dock with long strokes that cut the water. The water had cooled her rage, but the anger still simmered.

She pushed herself up and then sat, dripping, on the edge of the dock. A puddle formed around her. Peter sat a few feet away with his legs crisscrossed. She couldn't see him but could feel him watching her. He tapped his foot with nervous energy. It shook the whole dock. Shook her. Shook her mind. He expected her to say something. She had nothing to say. The weight of his expectation was too much. She could feel it pushing down on her. "Ugh!" she finally cried.

"Ugh," he said back.

She couldn't help it. She laughed a little. She looked over her shoulder. He was playing with his shoelaces. Anna was right next to him. Quiet.

"I can't send you home," she told them. "Even if I knew how, I don't have the magic. I shouldn't have called you here. I didn't know you'd bring your sister. If I could have warned you—"

"Don't worry about it," Peter said. His face told a different story.

"You said you saw a wolf?" Anna asked Harbor. "With the lady in the woods?"

"Yes," Harbor said.

"It's all mixed up," Anna said. "The wolf should have eaten the old lady, and an old lady in the woods should have tried to eat you. She'd draw you into her gingerbread and sugar-sweet cottage and fatten you up."

"The only one with a sweet cottage in the woods is Ruby, and she wouldn't eat anyone," Harbor told her.

"How long can we stay here?" Peter asked.

"You mean before The Frost come? I don't know." Harbor looked around. They would be safe there so long as they didn't draw attention to themselves. She wasn't sure if The Frost would consume the whole island or leave once they thought they'd taken everyone there. *Taken.* She had to use that word instead of *killed.* And then what? Would it be just the three of them alone on this island forever?

She couldn't, though. Peter and Anna were here because of her. It was her responsibility to get them back—or at least somewhere safe.

She stood up. "I'm going to go look for a chart," she said. "We can't stay here."

"What's a chart?" Anna asked.

"A map, but for out at sea. Frank taught me how to read them and how to navigate. I don't know if I can get you home, but I'll get you to safety. I promise."

If there was going to be a chart somewhere, the best bet would be at the harbormaster's office. Frank kept his office neat and tidy. She hoped who'd ever been stationed on this side had done the same.

Frank. She reached into her apron pocket. She still had the little figure he had made of her. She rubbed her finger over the figure's hair. Her hair. She tried not to cry.

She was nearly to the end of the dock when Anna called out. "Boat!"

Harbor turned around, already speaking. "That's impossible; there's no boat." But she looked where Anna was pointing, and indeed there was a small skiff. It headed straight for them.

CHAPTER TWENTY-SEVEN

Harbor hurried the others under the dock. They clung to one another, the water lapping at their ankles. Low tide, thankfully. The small boat was tied to the dock. Harbor held her breath. With her eyes, she urged Peter and Anna to do the same. She squeezed her bow.

Thunk. Thunk.

Footsteps on the wood planks shook the children to their cores.

A sliding sound. A body? A prisoner?

Anna squeezed her eyes closed.

"Come along then," a voice said. "We're home now, Mr. Broom. We'll have you in a warm bed soon enough."

Mr. Broom? That voice—was that Mr. Coffin?

Harbor poked her head out from under the dock. It was them!

"Mr. Coffin!" Harbor cried.

Mr. Coffin stumbled. He clutched Mr. Broom to him. With them were Mary and Hod Templeton. Hod had a cut on his arm that stained his shirt.

"Little girl, you nearly ended my life with fright. What are you doing down there?"

Harbor peeked under the dock and beckoned for Anna and Peter to come out. "I called him," she explained. "Sapphire told me to, and I did and we ran away and here we are."

"Good girl," Mary said. If she seemed disappointed that Peter was still a boy, she didn't say so.

"Harbor!" exclaimed Mr. Broom. "Did you see the elephants on your way over? I thought I saw one. Richie here tells me it was only a harbor seal, but I know an elephant from a harbor seal."

Harbor waded out from the water. "No, Mr. Broom, we didn't see any elephants."

"Come along," Mr. Coffin said. "Let's go to my store. I'll see what I've got to fix us up."

≈≈≈≈

After Mary and Mr. Coffin bandaged up Hod's arm at Mr. Coffin's store, the group went to the Templetons' old house and set Mr. Broom up in a well-worn armchair. Harbor made sure he had plenty of blankets and a glass of water. "You feel all right, Mr. Broom?"

"Never better," Mr. Broom said. "Always liked the way the moon fell on this side of the island. Could never get my

Claire to move to the North Village, though." He coughed and then looked at Harbor. "Such a blessing, you are. Never a curse. Not to me. Not to anyone who paid attention."

Mary soon had a fire burning in the fireplace, and they all sat around it. Even with the fire and the blankets, Mr. Broom shook with the cold.

"Not sure we'll ever be warm again," Hod said.

"Like frost on a window, they were. Subtle and fast," Mary said. "But not one speck beautiful."

Their harrowing tale came out in fits and starts as they settled in around the fire. They told of how wave upon wave of white soldiers crashed over their village and the people there. How the people they loved slipped away.

"Some they captured," Hod said, with a narrowing of his eyes. "The magic ones."

Harbor felt that like a punch in a stomach. *The magic ones.* He was saying something to her about her aunts, something she couldn't quite understand. All she could think was that if she had even one speck of magic, she'd be able to help her family and friends—and Peter and Anna. But she didn't.

They told Harbor how proud of her they were, how they were so glad to see she had called the hero and that he had come. That only made things worse. She had called the hero, but neither of them knew what to do.

"So, the bad guys are actual monsters?" Peter asked. "It's not just some scary name for them? Like Hydra or something. They're not just stone-cold killers? Which, you know, saying it out loud also sounds really bad."

"Mom says there's no such thing as monsters," Anna said.

"Mom also said there was no door to a magical world," Peter replied. "It must be hard to live in a place like this. Where the magical things are real. It's gotta be hard to tell what's real and what's a story. Like the giants you told me about. Were those really real?"

"Just a story Frank told me," Harbor said.

"Giants were as real as you or me," Mr. Broom said. "Like the elephants. Small Island used to be the Island of Giants, and there was so many of 'em that some of 'em had to live underground. This whole island is riddled with tunnels and caves. Why, once I was drilling a well and fell right in. Current picked me up and washed me out by the seal rocks."

Anna's eyes grew wide as Mr. Broom spoke. Harbor gave the girl a little shake of her head. It was just another of Mr. Broom's mixed-up stories.

"Don't shake your head at me, child. Those giants are as true as a baby washing up on the shore."

"Mr. Broom!" Mr. Coffin chided.

Hod looked over at Mr. Coffin. "'Bout time she heard, wouldn't you say?"

"Are we having a story?" Mr. Broom asked. "I do love a good story. Did I ever tell you about the elephant, Harbor?"

Harbor looked at Mr. Coffin. "We already figured it out. I'm the baby that washed up on the shore."

Mr. Coffin winced.

"We found the newspaper," Peter explained. "It was her, wasn't it?"

Mr. Coffin nodded.

Harbor could feel the tension, thick in the air like summer fog. "There's more, though? Isn't there?"

"I always told them that if you asked, I'd tell you," Mr. Coffin said.

He held her gaze for a long time, like he was testing her. Like he needed to be sure she really wanted to know. "Please," she whispered.

"All right, then. You know about our little cove where treasures—and heroes—come ashore. Sweet Harbor, we used to call it, but now it's simply The Place Where Things Wash Up. Of course, you've always known, Harbor, that some of those things came from The Somewhere Else. Like that strange device I found on your birthday."

"That was a phone, I think," Harbor said. "Peter has one in his pocket."

Peter pulled out his phone and showed Mr. Coffin. "Well, I'll be. A telephone that you carry with you?"

"Yeah, a cell phone. I think they used to call it a mobile phone? This one is a smartphone. It has data and you can get online and—"

Mr. Coffin shook his head. "You're decades ahead of me, I'm certain. I can't catch up on all of it this evening." He turned back to Harbor. "Part of my job, you see, was to make sure you never saw anything that would make you ask too many questions." He laced and unlaced his fingers nervously. "Dirigo Island, that's what we called it before, was always a special place. I always thought of it as a meeting place. A transfer station between two worlds."

"Like a sand bar, more like," Hod said. "Sometimes you can cross it, and sometimes it's covered by the tides."

"Truthfully, we never really knew how it worked," Mary said. "And we never asked many questions. For the most part, things functioned the way they ought to. If we got in a boat and headed west, well, we'd wind up on the mainland in the place you call The Somewhere Else. But sometimes there was strangeness."

"A boat might be lost; then the crew comes back years later, but decades older. Or not aged a day," Hod told them.

"Every generation, there was a boy or two who wanted to prove himself and sailed off in the highest of tides toward the place where the compass spins."

"That's what Frank's brother did, isn't it?" Harbor asked.

Mr. Coffin nodded. "Frank missed him every day."

Harbor moved closer and closer to Anna and Peter until the three were huddled together on the floor.

"And we had visitors!" Mary said. "Strange folk. Islanders loved their lore, and they believed in magic, and the blurriness didn't bother them much. People off the island thought us a little daft, but mainlanders always have their misconceptions about islanders. It went on like that for years. Times don't quite line up between the two worlds, and on the island, we seemed to fall somewhere in between. Islanders always lived longer than the mainlanders, and folks would say it was the clean, fresh air, but in truth it was because our time was moving more slowly."

Harbor was getting a sick feeling in her stomach.

Mr. Coffin picked up the tale. "We heard stories about Lapistyr. About the daughters of that realm, and how the youngest married a prince from another kingdom—oh the saga of it! We heard how they longed to have a baby, but to no avail." Mr. Coffin was silent for a moment. "I lived here, in the village on the north side of the island. I had a sister who I loved dearly. A younger sister. Like your Anna—such a light she was. She wanted to be a nurse. It was wartime, and nurses were needed. So she boarded the ferry back to the mainland—"

"A big storm blew in," Mary said softly.

"Yes," Mr. Coffin said. He breathed in deeply, as if at loss for air. "The ship was lost."

Mr. Coffin nodded. He was silent, staring at the wooden floor, unmoving. "I was standing on the shore. Hoping it was one of those times when the ship would come back with everyone on board. But instead, you washed up—" He was silent for so long that Harbor began to wonder if something had happened to him.

"This story doesn't add up," Peter said.

Harbor realized he was right. She had been born in Lapistyr and then brought to Small Island. "If I washed up here, how did I get to Lapistyr?"

Hod's face puckered so much that Harbor thought he

was going to spit. Mr. Coffin ran his hand through his hair. "A traveler was on the island through the storm—and when the baby washed up. A prince, he claimed to be, but I know a rapscallion when I see one, and that's what he was. Devious and sly, charming, but an oily kind of charming. I always assumed it was him who told the king and queen about the baby. They came within a fortnight."

"You have to understand, there was a war on," Mary said. "Coming closer every day."

"I knew it!" Peter said. "I read all about the U-boats off the coast of Maine."

Mr. Coffin nodded. "The king and queen offered to adopt the baby. By way of gratitude, they would protect the island. It all seemed such a wonderful plan. The islanders voted and it was settled. There was one problem, though."

"People talk too much," Hod said.

Mary shook her head, "We islanders have always loved to share a good yarn. They couldn't risk that. They offered us a choice: stay and stay forever, or leave and leave for good, a gold coin for each man, woman, and child who left. Many stayed. But for many, that gold coin was more money than they'd ever expect to see, and so they left."

"I think of those neighbors and friends often, the lives they must have led. But I'll never know." Mr. Coffin sighed.

"Why didn't you leave?" Harbor asked.

"He was hoping his sister would come back. Right?" Peter asked.

Mr. Coffin nodded. "Your aunts came to the island. The magic of those women, it was strong. Strong enough to move the island. They erased the thin spot—except for in one small stretch of land."

"The Place Where Things Wash Up," Harbor said.

"Then what happened?" Peter asked.

"The king and queen held a christening. It was a lovely affair, I am told. Until it came time for the blessings—well, you know all this. That's how you came back to the island."

"But why?" Harbor asked. "Why did they need a hidden place before I was even cursed?"

Mr. Coffin shrugged. "To protect us. That was the deal: a life free from war. Our little island had already lost so many boys who'd gone off to fight, first in the Great War and now in this one. They promised to insulate us from that threat."

"That makes sense," Peter said.

"After the curse, they needed a safe place for you, Harbor. So, you and your mother joined her sisters here."

"Who?" Harbor asked. "Who stayed? Who's from the other realm? The real world." The words tasted salty and hard in her mouth.

"Well, me, of course. Mr. Broom and Mary and Hod Templeton. Frank."

"What of the Murphys?" Harbor asked.

"They're nobles from Lapistyr, sent here as delegates."

It was all a play, each person playing their part to keep Harbor safe. Every single one had been lying to her for her entire life.

Anna tugged on her arm. "You could be from anywhere, Harbor. You could be from this realm or our realm or another one altogether."

Harbor jumped to her feet.

"Harbor?" Anna asked.

"I have to go," she said. "I need some air."

She ran toward the door. She heard Peter stand up behind her, but Mary said, "Stay." Peter stayed, and Harbor ran out into the night.

CHAPTER TWENTY-EIGHT

The waves lapped at Harbor's ankles. She'd always thought of this ocean as part of her. Salt in her hair, her skin, her blood. Blue churning water that kept her safe and restored her calm. Fish to feed her, wind to move her boat. She'd always known this, yet now she knew nothing. Maybe she had come, like Peter and Anna, from some landlocked place. Maybe the ocean did not care for her at all.

She reached her fingers to the sky. Amethyst had told her that the realms were like layers. Sapphire told her there were doors between them that were not really doors. Now Mr. Coffin had told her the whole island had shifted from one realm to another. What was true and what was real? She reached higher, as if she could touch the space between the realms and pull them back together.

But only a woman with strong magic could do that, and Harbor had none.

Harbor had no magic to save her friends from The Frost. She had no magic to send Peter and Anna home.

She did not know where she was from. She did not know who she was.

All she had was her hand in the sky.

She had nothing.

She *was* nothing.

Something burst against her fingers. Something cold, wet, and smelling of honeysuckle.

She yanked her hand back. Then, all around her, bubbles of water began to float. They sparkled in the moonlight just as they had on her birthday. Her heart caught in her throat. Could it be? Were her aunts here?

She spun around expecting to see them on the beach. No one was there. She clutched at her pendant filled with sand.

The bubbles burst at once, raining sweet water on her. All but one. It bounced along the shoreline, away from the village. Harbor followed it. It held the moonlight and glowed as it glided. Sometimes fast, sometimes slow. It went out around an outcropping of rocks. Harbor scrambled over them. It had to be her aunts. Or her mother! Oh, let it be her mother!

She was still furious at her mother, still weighed down with a huge sense of betrayal, but there was also no one else on earth she wanted to see more. Harbor climbed over the jetty. Her knee scraped barnacles.

She splashed onto the other side of the rocks, then froze.

On the beach sat the wolf.

"Awful late for a swim. Chilly, too."

Harbor spun around. The woman from the forest stood on the rocks, blocking her path back to the village. Harbor wanted to step away, but behind her was only ocean.

The woman moved toward Harbor, and for the first time, Harbor saw her fully. She had long, gray hair with strands of glittering silver woven through it. Her face was old and young at the same time. Her eyes flashed gray.

"You think you recognize me?" the woman asked.

Harbor nodded.

"It is because I am your aunt."

Harbor froze. She knew it was true. There was the slightly crooked mouth, the upturned nose, the bushy eyebrows that tied her aunts and mother together. "Micah," she said.

"Yes."

Now Harbor did scramble backward, wading all the way to her knees. She had left her bow back at the Templetons'. How foolish!

"Peace, child." Micah's crooked mouth made a smile.

"What do you want from me? Have you come to see the damage you have wrought?"

"The damage I have wrought?" Micah laughed. "Oh, child, you are misled. Or foolish. I hope you are not foolish." She sat on a rock at the edge of the sea.

"You cursed me. You said I'd prick my finger and that would make a war come."

"Is that what I said?" Micah asked. She reached up and began braiding her own hair. The silver strands sparkled in the night. "Your mother was such a beautiful baby. Fat and happy. Always laughing."

Harbor wondered if she could race past Micah. But no, Micah had magic on her side.

For her part, Micah seemed not bothered at all. "When it came time for her to go out into the world and find her husband, I had my eye on a farmer for her. Potatoes, I think it was. He was fat and happy, too. Your mother, though, such a flare for the dramatic. For romance. So, when your father caught her on the pier that day, the poor old potato farmer lost his shot at being king and Lapistyr started to fall."

A larger wave smacked against Harbor, soaking her to the middle of her back. She was a good swimmer. Perhaps she could swim out and around and back to safety.

"Come in from the water. I won't hurt you, child. I never meant you any harm."

Harbor did not move except to shiver in the cold. She could not run, so she had to stand her ground. She jutted out her chin and straightened her spine. "You make no sense. How could my mother meeting my father start the fall of Lapistyr?"

"Ah, there's the problem."

Another wave hit Harbor.

"Really, child, I won't hurt you. I swear by all the stones of Lapistyr."

Harbor eased her way out of the water, but still did not come too close to Micah.

"The history was not told to you, I suspect," Micah said. "The history of your father's land is an angry and sad one, and everyone was bent on protecting you at all costs. They never wanted you to feel uncomfortable."

Harbor scowled, and that made Micah laugh. "You look like your mother. It took a lot to get her riled, but once she was, my oh my, you had better watch yourself." She tossed her braid over her shoulder. "As I was saying, before your father's kingdom was Benspeir, it was another kingdom."

"The Kingdom That Was. I know," Harbor said.

"You know everything then." Micah stood. "It seems you don't need my help at all."

"I don't," Harbor said.

The wolf walked past Harbor and sat by Micah's side.

"Those are pretty trinkets around your neck," Micah said.

Harbor's hand went to her chest to cover them.

"Sand from Lapistyr from your mother, a glass from Sapphire. That clip in your hair must be from Amethyst."

Micah reached into the folds of her cloak. "I suppose I should add to your charms. I am your aunt, too, after all."

"I want nothing from you!" Harbor cried.

Micah crouched. She left something golden and round on the rocks. "Some stories need to be told, Harbor." She turned to go, then paused and looked back over her shoulder. "I have been wondering, what did you ever decide to do with that fish?"

Harbor must have looked confused. Micah said, "The fish you and Frank caught—your queening lesson. Being a royal woman of Lapistyr truly is filled with impossible choices. Why, you have one in front of you right now."

"What do you mean?" Harbor said, backing up again.

"Are you going to try to bring your new friends back home or rescue the old ones?"

Harbor felt tears welling.

"You are frightened," Micah said.

"I'm not!" Harbor wiped snot from beneath her nose.

"You are. As you should be. Our people are in danger."

"*Our* people? You betrayed us all years ago!"

"So it would seem to those who don't know the whole story, but I promise you I love Lapistyr and I love your aunts every bit as much as you do. Probably more. It's why I warned them, not that it mattered. It's why I'm here now."

"Then save them!" Harbor took a few quick steps toward Micah. "You have magic! You can save them!"

"I'm afraid that's not my role. Only a child of Benspeir can stop this."

"How can I fight The Frost? There are so many of them and only one of me!"

"Who said anything about fighting?"

"It's a war," Harbor replied.

"The hero brings the war's end. Isn't that what Amethyst promised?"

Of course. Micah wasn't trying to be helpful. She only wanted to insult her sisters.

Micah smiled. "It is your choice, Harbor Rose. Blessings and curses, they are not fates. You still have a choice in all this. I hope you make the right one."

"You hope I make the one *you* think is right," Harbor said.

"Perhaps you are not so foolish after all." Micah swung her cloaks around her and was gone over the rocks, the wolf loping behind.

There was a grunting and the sound of pebbles splashing into the water, and then Peter heaved himself up on the rocks. "Holy moly, who was that?"

"My aunt," Harbor said. "The one that cursed me."

"Whoa," Peter said. "Was that a wolf with her? Is that her familiar? Is she—" He saw Harbor's face, and he stopped talking. "Sorry," he whispered. He stepped closer to her and held out a hand that found its way to her shoulder and gave her a gentle pat. "What did she want?"

"She told me a bunch of nonsense about my father's kingdom." Harbor's voice was laced with venom. She wanted to spit the words from her mouth. Her father was one of the bravest and noblest of men ever to have lived. Her father held no guilt or shame. Her father . . . may not actually be her father.

If the basic truths of her life were wrong, what did she really know?

"She said it was my father's people that caused this. That and my parents falling in love. At least, I think that's what she said. Everything's a jumble."

"You're telling me," Peter said. "This morning I was in the office for fighting, and now I'm here and nothing makes sense."

He sat on the rocks and pulled his knees to his chest. Harbor sat beside him. "I'm really sorry I called you. If I knew everything I know now—or what I didn't know. If I thought—" She stopped. "I'm just really sorry."

He picked up a pebble and tossed it into the ocean. *Plink.* "Not as sorry as me," he said. "I keep going over it in my head. *Why me? Why me?* I'm no hero, Harbor."

"You're a fighter. You just told me as much."

Plink, plink—two more pebbles into the sea. "Yeah, about that. I let my dad and everyone think I got into a fight, but really I just muttered something stupid and Cam heard me and jumped me. I don't think I even got one punch in."

Plink. Plink.

"According to Micah, you don't need to fight to win a war."
Plink.

"But you do need to fight to keep your face out of the toilet," he said.

Plink. Plink.

"Wait!" Harbor slapped her hand on Peter's wrist.

In his palm was the small sphere that Micah had left behind. "Don't touch that!"

"Why not? What is it?" Panicked, he dropped the ball.

She caught it in her free hand. It thrummed in her grasp. The world went dark, and she and Peter fell into a dream.

CHAPTER TWENTY-NINE

They stood on barren land, but it was only empty for a moment. Trees sprouted around them. Leaves first, then tiny saplings, then wide-trunked trees that swayed in the wind. The biggest of all was a plumrose tree whose bark was black as coal. The blossoms bloomed deep purple, and then bright red fruit emerged. The fruit fell; more trees grew. Thousands and thousands of plumrose trees. Faster and faster, the changes came. Then there were people. They dressed in rich purples and greens with intricate embroidery. Harbor saw the stories on their pant legs and sleeves but could not tell them to Peter. They could only watch. The people tended the trees, culling only as many as they could grow back. At first. But then the people cut more and more trees. Trunks fell all around Peter and Harbor. They huddled together.

Soon, all that was left was a single plumrose tree. A young man with a crown on his head stood at the base of the tree.

He ordered a limb cut. Then another. Cut after cut was taken until all that was left was a stump. Then the man with the crown ordered that pulled out, too.

From the hole where the tree had been, it emerged. Slow at first, then faster and faster. The Frost. It moved like a sickness, person to person. Once struck by the illness, the person was no longer wholly themselves. They were part of The Frost.

Those who survived tried to fight. Soldiers from the Soth lands arrived wearing metal armor and carrying swords. They fought against The Frost. Lives were lost on both sides. Then a small boy appeared. A flash of light. The Frost lay on the ground.

Three women with flowing gowns and flowing hair descended from the sky. Each held a stone: emerald, agate, garnet. The woman who held the emerald closed her eyes. She touched the shoulder of one woman, then the other. They made a circle around the hole where the tree had grown and swayed together. The Frost was pulled from the bodies. Some specks turned into waspgulls. Other white dust went into the ground.

Gone.

Another boy with a crown emerged. He dropped a seed into the ground. A new plumrose tree grew, but only one. Around it sprouted gray-barked ash trees. People, too. Kings and princes one generation after the next until . . .

Harbor gasped.

"What was that?" Peter demanded. "What happened?"

She squeezed the ball in her hand. "This object is cursed. It can't be. It can't—"

"Was that a dream? Did we time travel?"

"It was nothing. A mirage."

But it felt real.

The man at the end had been her father, young, proud, and true, leaving the land in a ship.

↝↝↝↝

Harbor and Peter crouched together in the doorway of Mr. Coffin's store. After this vision, Harbor hadn't wanted to go back to the Templetons' house, not until she figured out what to do.

"You think that was history?" Peter asked.

"I'm not sure." Some of the story matched what she had heard, but she had always been told that her father's people had been sailors who had discovered an abandoned city, one ravaged by greed, and made it their own. They had planted the gray-barked ash trees, according to legend—the ones that brought them wealth and the ones for which her father had been named. The vision told her that they had not discovered the land at all. They had been the ones to destroy it and then buried their shame. "I don't think my father—" she began. She wasn't sure what to think.

"I'm just thinking that if someone got it into the ground before, maybe we can get it into the ground again. The women who did it—those were magical women from Lapistyr, right?"

"I have no magic," Harbor reminded him.

"I know, but Hod said the magic ones weren't taken over, so if we could rescue them, then maybe they could put it back in the ground."

His shoulder was pressed against hers, solid as a rock.

"But you and Anna—"

"The only sure way to get back is if your aunts send us. Unless you think you can convince wolf lady to help us, your aunts are our only choice."

"They might not be my aunts."

"Maybe not by blood," Peter said. "But I'm not sure if that matters."

Harbor wasn't sure if it did either. She wished that she had heard the story from her parents, though. Now she wasn't sure who she was. She might not be a true princess. She might not even be from this realm. All those ideas of who she was that were once locked in stone now felt uncertain.

"Here's what I'm thinking: monsters tend to have rules. And weaknesses." He sighed. "If this were D&D, I would know exactly what to do. I feel like we need to do some more research before we can make a plan."

"There's no time for research," Harbor said. "We know that they spread and infect and take over the minds and bodies of those they touch. I watched it happen to Frank. Eventually, they destroy the land. They destroy everything. That's their only goal."

"So just your average, everyday supervillain," Peter said dryly. "Cool, cool, cool."

The sky was starting to get lighter. Morning was breaking. "I wonder what the sunrise is like on this side of the island," Harbor said.

"You've got to focus, Harbor. I guess we can figure out The Frost's weakness and how we can use it to rescue your aunts later. First, we need to figure out how to get back."

Harbor pressed her face against her knees. "You don't have to do this. You don't have to be our hero."

"If I want to get me and Anna home, I kind of do," he said. "Anyway, that's sort of the whole hero deal. The hero always refuses the call at first. I'm just hoping that this is the darkest hour point, because I don't think I can stand for things to get much worse."

He stood, then reached down to help her to her feet. "Milady," he said, then turned red as a plumrose blossom.

Harbor was well trained by Leo. She curtsied and said, "'Twould be my honor if you accompanied me on this journey." She smiled at him.

"So, we're doing this?" Peter said. "Save the magic ladies, defeat The Frost, and then go home. That's the plan?"

"It's not precisely a plan," Harbor said.

"It normally takes me weeks to plan a campaign when I'm the DM. A not-precisely-a-plan plan might be the best I can do on short notice."

Harbor said, "There are two ways back to the other side of the island. By land or by boat."

"Boat, I guess. I'm not much of a hiker. You get the boat ready, and I'll tell Anna and the others what we're doing."

She still felt hesitant. Had she thought through all the options? All the possible outcomes? Was this Opal Pearl's birthday blessing? Opal Pearl had given her a dash of reason, but to Harbor it felt like indecision. "Right now?" she asked. "Maybe we should think a little more."

"No time like the present to start a mission that's almost certainly doomed to fail."

"Peter!"

"Sorry! When I get extra, extra nervous, I tend to go grim." He shrugged. "Meet you at the dock."

Harbor thought that perhaps she ought to be the one to tell the others of her plan, but she was afraid they would try to talk her out of it. Peter was the hero, and they would trust him.

The skiff the others had come in was in better shape than the old boat they'd taken from The Place Where Things Wash Up. It had a sail, too, which would make the traveling easier. She tucked her bow and arrows into a cubby near the stern. As she sat back up, the glass Sapphire had given her swung forward. The morning light caught it and cast a rainbow on the bottom of the boat. A good omen, she hoped.

She lifted the glass to her eye. How strange! All the color drained from the world around her. Except for the boat itself. *To see the path.* Her aunts had known she would need these gifts—the dash of reason, the lens to see, bravery, and perseverance. But, if they had known she would need these gifts, why had they not helped her to avoid the situation altogether?

Why hadn't they stopped The Frost?

Why had they kept so many secrets?

CHAPTER THIRTY

Ahoy, matey!" Peter called from the end of the dock. He smiled, but even from a distance, Harbor could tell it was forced. Anna was with him. "We've had a slight change of plans," he explained. "This one won't stay put."

Anna said, "I can be a hero, too."

There was no time for argument. The siblings got in first and Harbor pushed off. The water shimmered, reflecting the low-hanging sun. There was a chill in the air and bit of fog in the distance.

Frank had taught her to sail so long ago she hardly remembered learning. But thinking of it made her think of all the people who had helped to raise her—and how they were all trapped by The Frost. It was easy to forget on such a beautiful morning, but Harbor forced herself to remember. Mr. Coffin and the others were counting on them to complete this mission. Maybe she should have said goodbye to them, but just the thought made her heart hurt too much.

"We'll stay close to the shore," she said. "Anna, keep an eye out for rocks and ledges so we can steer around them."

"Aye, aye, Captain!" Anna replied. She gave a little salute and then leaned out onto the point of the stern to watch the water move around them.

"You're a living figurehead," Harbor told her.

"A what?" Anna asked.

"The figure on the front of a boat," Harbor explained.

"It's usually a mermaid," Peter added. "For luck. It's kind of funny, actually, because mermaids were supposed to be bad luck and so was having women on boats. But, mermaids, you know, don't wear shirts, and so having a mermaid on there, without a shirt, it was supposed to calm the sea gods and that would make for a safe journey home."

"Encyclopedia mouth," Anna said.

It was strange how some things were alike and some quite different. Lapistyr's ships had waspgulls on the front, a nod to her father's homeland. Their sharp beaks, carved of mahogany, pointed out across the water. Oh, how Harbor wished to see one of those ships now!

Or perhaps she did not. She could not shake what Micah had shown her about her father's people. Greedy and violent, never satisfied with what they had, they desired for more, more, more and it was bringing about the wreck of the world.

A strip of land stuck out from the island, and Harbor navigated around it.

"Puffins!" Anna cried.

A gaggle of puffins sat on the rocks, their fat bellies

sticking out almost as far as their orange beaks. "I never thought I'd see a puffin in real life and oh!" Anna sat up so suddenly the boat rocked back and forth.

"Easy there," Harbor said.

"But it's a seal! Look, Peter, a seal!"

The seal turned its shiny head to look at them. *Arf!* it called. Anna clapped her hands together.

"I remember what you told me about seals," Harbor said. "About how seals and their mothers have special calls so the mother can find the pup when she got back from hunting."

"I told you that?" Peter asked.

"Yes, the first time you came."

The seal dove underwater, then resurfaced again farther on. Dove and resurfaced. Dove and—nothing.

"Where'd it go?" Anna asked.

"Seals can stay underwater a long time," Harbor told her.

They could still hear the seal, though, barking from someplace they couldn't see.

They were edging dangerously close to the cliffs that were covered over with strands of ivy that swayed in the breeze.

"Huh," Peter said. "Look how the ivy there is going back and forth."

"So?" Anna asked.

"The ivy on either side, it's not moving like that." Peter grabbed Harbor's arms. "The giants, Harbor!"

"I told you there's no such thing as giants."

Just as she said it, the wind blew all the ivy aside and revealed an opening in the cliff.

CHAPTER THIRTY-ONE

The walls wept water over green algae. Peter touched the stone, then pulled his hand back. They had navigated the sailboat to the mouth of the cave and now stood on a ledge inside.

"It can't be," Harbor said. "I always thought the giants and their tunnels were just legends."

They made their way deeper into the cave toward a glowing light. Their shoulders bumped as they walked. When they got closer to the glow, they saw a set of stairs that sparkled as if someone had dropped golden dust on them. "They're yellow brick road stairs," Anna said. Seeing that Harbor was confused, she said, "Like in *The Wizard of Oz*."

"I don't think they have *The Wizard of* Oz here," Peter said.

"Dorothy had to follow the yellow brick road to get to Oz to go home. There was a wizard there. Well, he was supposed to be a wizard. Really, he was a fake," Anna explained.

"Spoiler!" Peter cried. "She might watch it someday."

Harbor ran her hand over the lowest step. The algae was slippery, and the stone looked ready to crumble. Each step was nearly as tall as her. Up, up, up, they went, to a small patch of light.

"The Giants' Stairs go into the woods, right?" Peter asked.

Harbor nodded. "We could go up. I know you wanted to sail, but this could be a safer way to approach the village, less chance of being spotted by scouts." It was a long way up, but they could do it. Or so she hoped.

"Mr. Broom said he rode the current to the seal rocks," Peter said. "Would that be faster?"

"But if we pop out on the rocks, The Frost might be there. We might not have any cover," Harbor said. "This is safer."

She reached up and gripped the top. With her feet, she scrambled up.

"Listen," Peter said. "I'm just not sure I'm going to be able to do these stairs."

"He's afraid of heights," Anna said.

"I suffer from slight acrophobia," Peter confirmed. "Though, it's really more a fear of falling."

Harbor tried to hide her disappointment. Their hero was too young, untrained, and, it seemed, full of fears.

"I wish there was a way to tell which way was better," Anna said. "The tunnel or the stairs."

Harbor realized that perhaps there was. She held her lens from Sapphire to her eye.

"Is that some kind of magic marble?" Peter asked.

"Sapphire gave it to me so I could see the way ahead."

She scanned the cave. The stairs glowed. "We have to—"
But as she turned to look at the others, the tunnel glowed,
too. "They both glow."

"They're both the right path?" Anna asked.

"How do we choose?" Peter said.

Harbor wasn't sure.

"The yellow brick road got them to Oz, but it wasn't a
safe journey," Anna said.

"True," Peter agreed. "And from Mr. Broom, we know
you can get through those tunnels okay."

"Is that your choice?" Harbor asked.

"My choice?" Peter replied.

"You're the hero," she told him.

He hesitated. "Then yes, that's my choice."

The three climbed back in the boat. Harbor made sure
the sail was tied tight against the boom and the boom was
locked in its place. They had no need of sails. The water
would carry them where they needed to go.

Anna took her place at the front. "You're our eyes," Harbor said.

"I have a light," Peter said. "Hod gave it to me. It's an old
flashlight." He handed it to Anna, who nodded seriously. She
grasped the light in both hands and pointed it straight ahead.

The wet walls dripped.

The water moved along like a river, and they didn't have

to paddle much. Mostly they used the oars to keep themselves going straight. Occasionally they bumped into the edge of the tunnel with a scraping noise.

"How far below the earth do you think we are?" Peter asked.

Harbor didn't know. They had gone in under the high side of the island, so the earth likely stretched hundreds of feet above them.

"Do you think giants really made these tunnels? They don't seem very high."

"Maybe they floated in them like a lazy river," Anna suggested. She pointed the light upward. The ceiling of the tunnel was only a few feet over their heads.

Peter sucked in a deep breath. "I guess I'm claustrophobic, as well as acrophobic."

The walls here were smoother than they had been at the tunnel's opening. Harbor reached out and let her fingers drift across the smooth stone. Every few feet, a round knob of rock stuck out. "I wonder what those are," she said.

"It's eerie in here," Anna said. "Like a ride at a carnival. A scary one."

"This is no ride," Peter said. "Nothing's going to jump out at us."

As they went on, the ceiling got lower and lower.

"I don't like this," Peter said. "This couldn't possibly be a giant's tunnel. We went the wrong way. We should go back. Go around."

"We can't," Harbor said. "The current is too strong."

The ceiling was only a foot above their heads now. Water dripped on them like rain. Peter swiped it from his face.

"Close your eyes," Harbor said. "Just close your eyes. We'll be through soon." In truth Harbor had no idea where they were. Her own heart raced as did her mind.

"I made the wrong choice," Peter said.

The ceiling lowered even more.

Anna moved to the bottom of the boat. Harbor and Peter did the same. It was damp, and the water soaked through their clothes until they were chilled to the bone.

Still the tunnel tightened.

Peter's breath came in quick gasps. Anna grasped his hands. Harbor closed her eyes.

Lower still.

They crouched together, practically lying on the bottom of the skiff. Anna's head was on Peter's leg. Peter and Harbor curled toward each other like snails.

"Breathe," Harbor whispered. Harbor used to get so worked up about every little thing. The rain came on a day she wanted to play outside. Her weaving was lopsided, and she had to undo it and do it again. She bit into a sour blueberry. Her little face would pinch up and go red. Her mother would grip her hands and say, "Breathe, Harbor. Just breathe." Harbor's mother would breathe out calm that Harbor sucked in. That was her magic. Harbor wished she had that magic to help Peter and Anna. More than that, she wished her mother were there now, to hold her hand and make her feel safe.

The ceiling was so low the sides of the boat scraped. Harbor reached up. She used her hands to push them along. Faster, faster. If this tunnel ended deep under the island, just slanted to nothingness, better to know sooner.

The air felt heavy and cold at once. Like there wasn't enough of it.

She kept pushing them on, on, on.

All at once, the world filled with light.

Harbor blinked against the brightness.

"What—" Peter began.

They were in the middle of an azure lagoon. Cliff walls went up, up, up, where they were greeted by trees. Three other tunnels opened at the four compass points, each a different size.

"It's a crossroads," Harbor said.

Peter gasped air as though he would never get enough. He held his hand to his chest.

Anna looked around. "It's beautiful," she said. "Do you think anyone else has ever been here? Anyone else in the history of the world?"

"Well, not from your world, I should think," Harbor said. "But this one—the giants most definitely came here. Maybe people, too."

"It feels like no one has ever been here," Anna said.

Harbor carefully lifted herself onto the seat. Peter pulled

himself up beside her. His hands shook. "Now what?" he asked.

Harbor pointed to the tunnel directly across from where they had popped out. "Assuming the tunnels are straight, that one will lead us right out under the fort, so we don't want that one." She pointed to the one to the east. "If Mr. Broom really did wash up where the seals gather, then we want to go east. The westerly one might be all right, too."

Peter chewed the skin of his thumb. "Please don't ask me to make this choice," he told her. "I royally messed up the last one."

"Not necessarily," Harbor said. "We are making our way through the island."

Their little boat rocked back and forth.

"East or west?" she asked him.

"Go west, young man," Peter said. Then he laughed. "That's something my dad always says. I'm not sure why. I looked it up, and it was something this guy Horace Greeley said. It was about western expansion, and he was encouraging young men to go west and build new lives there and expand the country. It wasn't great, actually—"

"Peter," Anna said softly.

"I know, I know. Encyclopedia mouth."

"I say we go for the east," Anna said. "That's where the seals are, and a seal helped us find the tunnel."

"We're really going to trust the seals?" Peter asked. "I'm

starting to think they are rascally little creatures. Seals are the raccoons of the ocean world."

Harbor ignored Peter. "Why don't we row over and take a look at the eastern tunnel? If it looks okay, we'll take that one. If not, we'll check out the western one."

"But not the northern one," Peter said.

"Right. The northern one leads right to danger," Harbor said.

"Process of elimination. We've got this," Peter said.

Harbor and Peter picked up their oars. They spun the boat in the direction of the eastern tunnel, planning to cut across the lagoon.

"You know, aside from the whole peril and perhaps never being able to see our families again, this is pretty cool," Peter said as he dipped his oar into the water. "An underground lagoon? I mean, objectively speaking, that's pretty awesome. I'd rather have seen it under other—"

Peter's words were swallowed by the sound of rushing water. The boat was pulled into a spiral. The lagoon's waters swirled around.

"A whirlpool?!" he cried. "Are we trapped in an underground whirlpool?"

"Hold on!" Harbor yelled.

The boat spun faster and faster.

The walls around them blurred. The water, too.

"Peter!" Anna called.

Peter dove onto the bottom of the boat. He held his sister in place.

Bang! The boat shot forward. Harbor gripped her seat.

The boat blasted into the tunnel on the northern side of the lagoon. Before they could even scream, they were falling.

CHAPTER THIRTY-TWO

Harbor's stomach lodged in her throat. Peter's hands scrambled for purchase. Anna curled herself into a tight little ball.

Splash!

The boat hit the water. Their bodies slammed against the bottom of the boat.

Their screams echoed around the tunnel. The current carried them along so quickly that wind whipped Harbor's hair into her face. Peter and Anna clung to each other.

Harbor tried to get her bearings. They were going too fast. If she tried to stop them with the oar, it would snap. A rope, maybe? One of her arrows? She looked through her marble lens. Nothing.

If only Frank were here. He'd know how to tame this boat!

He'd told her to let the boat go where it wanted, true. But she'd also seen him guide a boat against its will.

Look. Pay attention.

It was Frank's voice in her head.

Her knuckles were white as she gripped the seat. She turned her head first one way, then the other.

The tunnel was wide. The raging current went down the center. On either side, the flow was softer.

She needed to get them out of the swift current. If she did it too quickly, they might break apart or smash against the side of the tunnel.

She remembered how Frank reeled the big fish in. Pull in a little. Let them pull back. Each time, pulling the fish a little closer.

"Peter," she said. He couldn't hear her. The wind was too loud.

They jolted over something. Anna screamed. Harbor's stomach retched.

"Peter!" she yelled.

He looked at her over his shoulder.

"You two need to do what I say exactly when I say it."

Peter looked at Anna. His face was as pale as a crab's belly. Peter shook his head.

"You have to," she said. She fought to keep the quaver from her voice.

Anna looked up.

Harbor explained her plan. "I'm going to need you to shift your weight around. Front, back, right, and left."

Anna nodded, but her lip quivered.

"Move back with me. Against the bench."

The siblings eased themselves back. The bow lifted.

"On my mark, go to the front."

Harbor dropped her oar into the starboard side and held it firm. The bow turned. "Now!"

They crawled to the bow. The current caught the bow and they fishtailed.

"Too slow!" Harbor said. "You have to move quickly."

"Harbor, I can't," Peter said.

"You have to."

"I'm scared."

"So am I, but if we don't do this—we have to do this."

Anna took her brother's hand. "We can do this. Let's try again."

Anna and Peter moved back by Harbor. She put her oar in again. She waited until the bow crested the wake of the current. "Now!"

This time, the siblings leaped to the front of the boat. The bow dipped into the slower part of the current. Harbor whipped her oar around to the other side.

They straightened out.

"To the right!" she cried.

Anna and Peter rolled to the right. The boat tipped back in that direction.

"Left!" she yelled.

They jiggled back and forth like that, to the right and then a correction until the boat was in the slower current.

"Okay," Harbor said.

Her hands were raw, and sweat dripped off her face. The boat, though, was safe.

෨෨෨෨

Once they had slowed down, they could look around. The walls were decorated with symbols: swirls and wreaths and barbs that crossed. "Can you read that?" Peter asked Harbor.

"No," Harbor said. "Maybe it's just a design."

The little flashlight didn't do much to cut the darkness, and the symbols were hard to see. They drifted on. Harbor made sure they didn't slip back into the rapids.

"How'd you know how to do that?" Peter asked.

"Frank," Harbor told him.

"Wish I'd had a Frank," Peter said. He sat on the bottom of the boat, knees drawn to his chest. "Boats, tunnels, darkness—none of this is exactly my strong suit."

Harbor wasn't sure what to say to that. She, too, wished she had been sent a hero better suited to the challenge. But the hero you get is the hero you have, and she was going to need Peter at his best to take down The Frost.

"You did great," she told him. "Just fine."

Peter shook his head. They floated on in silence.

"I think," Anna said after a piece. "I think it's getting lighter ahead."

Harbor picked up the oars. She rowed toward the light. As she did, the sounds of the ocean came to them: waves crashing and seagulls calling. Faster they rowed until they no longer needed the light. On and on until the wild ocean opened in front of them. Harbor pulled the boat over to the side of the tunnel. A metal post was driven into the rocks as if just waiting for a boat to be tied there.

One at a time, they climbed onto the ledge.

"Ah, land," Peter cried. "Sweet land. Never again will I take you for granted. Rocks, how I love thee. Let me count the ways. First, you are solid. Second, you are not an angry, raging current."

Harbor inched her way along the ledge until she was at the mouth of the cave. Waves lapped at the cliff, which dropped a few feet before hitting the ocean and then stretched another twenty feet above it. She couldn't see the fort itself, but she could see white and red flags billowing in the breeze. She wanted to snatch them and send them to the bottom of the ocean.

"I have some good news and some bad news."

"Of course," Peter said. "Never a good news, good news situation."

"Better than a bad news, bad news situation," Anna told him.

"I know where we are. We are right under the fort, more or less."

"That's the bad news," Peter said. "What's the good news?"

"No, that was the good news. I know where we are. The bad news is, to get away from here, we're going to have to climb along the cliff."

CHAPTER THIRTY-THREE

Did I say I love rocks?" Peter asked. His fingertips were white as he dug into the stone face of the cliff. "I hate rocks. I hate rocks and I hate heights, and, honestly, I'm starting to hate the ocean."

"Don't look down," Harbor said.

When one is told not to do something, it's nearly impossible to comply. Peter looked down. The whole world spun.

"Are you going to barf?" Anna asked. "He barfed on Dragon's Descent, and they had to close the whole ride. It landed on some lady's hair."

"Anna!" Peter cried. "Do you always have to tell that story?"

Having never had a sibling, Harbor wasn't sure why they were choosing this moment to bicker. "We'll just take it nice and slow," Harbor said. Her bow was slung across her chest and scraped the rocks as she moved.

Harbor had gone first out onto the cliff. There was a ledge about a foot deep, though in some places it narrowed. Next came Anna and then Peter. They inched their way along the cliff face.

"How far is it we have to go?" Peter asked, trying to make his voice sound calm.

"I'm not exactly—"

"Approximately?"

Harbor realized that it didn't matter much what she answered, so she said, "Oh, just a bit more. Not even twenty-five yards." She hoped it was close to true. She knew the cliff bent around the northwest side of the island. She just hoped they'd find a way up before they got all the way around to The Place Where Things Wash Up.

Harbor took another step. The rock crumbled beneath it. She grasped for purchase in the stone in front of her. Her elbow grazed the rock. She winced.

"Are you okay?" Anna asked.

"What?" Peter demanded. "What happened?"

He'd been staring at the cliff face, but now, slowly, turned his head. The rock next to Harbor had given way, leaving a three-foot gap in the ledge.

"Oh no, oh no," Peter said, swaying from side to side.

There was nowhere else to go. No way back. No way around.

Harbor's elbow throbbed, but she reached her arm over the gap. A bit of stone jutted out. She gripped it, then extended her leg. One foot over. Her body hung out over open space. Nothing but the sea below. She squeezed her eyes shut. *It's up to you, Harbor.*

Moving carefully, she pulled her other leg over. She let out her breath.

She'd had to stretch her legs to cover the space. Would Anna be able to make it?

"I've got this," Anna said, her little face set firmly. She reached out a hand. Harbor took it and placed it on the handhold.

"One foot first," Harbor said.

Anna reached out her leg. Her toes nearly touched the other side.

Harbor gripped Anna's wrist. "You're going to have to trust yourself. And me."

"What do you want me to do?" Anna asked. Her voice was small, but solid.

"Push off. Take the step."

Anna looked right into Harbor's eyes.

"I won't let you fall. I promise."

Anna stepped. Just as her left foot lifted, her right foot landed. Harbor pulled her in tight.

There was enough space for Anna to slide around Harbor on the ledge.

"Now it's your turn," Harbor said to Peter.

"Yeah, you know, I'm good right here," Peter said.

"You can't just stay on the cliff, Peter," Anna told him.

"Reach your hand out," Harbor said. "I'll help you get the handhold. You don't even need to open your eyes."

Peter didn't move. "I can't. It's too far." His voice quavered. Tears burned his eyes. He blazed with humiliation. He was the oldest. He ought to be leading, yet here he was clinging to the cliff like a bird in a storm.

"You can," Harbor told him.

He only shook his head.

"He's really afraid of heights," Anna said softly.

Harbor stepped back over the opening with one foot. Peter's breath was ragged. Sweat dotted his brow even though the air was chilled.

"Okay," she said. "We can do this."

Harbor touched her chest, right where Sapphire had touched her when she'd blessed her with a drop of bravery. She felt a tingling in her hand. Without thinking about it, she placed her hand on Peter's arm. A shock crackled through her fingers and onto his skin.

He breathed in, sharp and deep. "What was—" he began. But then, he reached out.

Harbor took his hand. She stepped back over. She placed his hand on the hold. "Now your right foot," she said.

His leg shook. As he pulled himself over, his shirt rose and the granite scraped the skin on his soft belly. He winced but kept going until he was on the other side. He clung to the rock and breathed heavily.

"You did it!" Anna cheered.

"You okay?" Harbor asked. "Can you keep going?"

Peter nodded. They kept inching along in their new order: Anna, then Harbor, then Peter. When Peter began to shake, Harbor would touch him lightly and that same sizzle snapped from her hand to him.

After what seemed like ages, Harbor noticed trees growing out of the cliff face. The pines held on like barnacles, and their roots provided a ladder. "We go up here," she said.

Anna scrambled up.

"Do you want to go before me?" Harbor asked.

"You going to catch me? I'd take us both down," Peter said. But he started climbing.

Harbor waited until he was halfway up before she started her own climb. Her hands grew sticky with pine pitch. The smell was as familiar to her as the sea.

When Peter reached the top, he climbed on his hands and knees, then flopped over onto his back.

Harbor crawled up next to him and got her bearings. They were in a bit of scrubland above the cliff. Smoke drifted from the fort and blew toward them. That was good. That meant any sound they made would be carried away from the fort as well. There were no paths up here, but Harbor knew the way across the fields. It was dangerous, but if they stayed close to the ground, they could make it.

"No one back home would believe it, Peter," Anna said. "You and me, rock climbing a cliff above the ocean! Without ropes! It's gotta be three times as high as the wall at The Summit."

Harbor watched them. They had their own language. Not just the words, but the memories.

Anna turned to Harbor. "When Peter was seven, he went to a birthday party at this rock gym and he got scared and the girl working there had to climb up and like carry him down."

"Anna!" Peter said. "You were a *baby* then. You don't even remember." He sat up.

"It's like I remember," Anna said. "That's almost as good."

Peter scowled. "What now?"

"We need to find a safe place. We can't easily get to the woods from here, but we can get to Opal Pearl's cottage. If it's still there."

"Well, let's go." Peter stood and wiped his brow with his wrist. His whole face was as tight as a sail on a windy day. "Sooner we get this done, sooner we can go home." He marched away from them.

"You don't even know where you're going!" Harbor called after him.

Peter didn't look back. His back was stiff. He kicked at stones as he walked, fists clenched.

"He gets like this sometimes. Mom says it's when he's embarrassed," Anna said.

"There's nothing to be embarrassed about," Harbor said.

Anna shrugged. "Best to give him his space."

"We don't have time for that," Harbor said. She chased after him at a trot, Anna with her. They quickly caught up to him.

"Wait," she said. "You don't know the way."

He stopped and spun around. "You're right. I don't. I don't know the way, and I don't know how to save your people, and I don't know how to get me and Anna back! I don't know why I was chosen as a hero. I don't know anything!"

Harbor put her hand on his shoulder. "I know what it's like to feel like you were supposed to be something," she said. "I was supposed to have magic."

Peter stared at his feet.

Harbor continued, "We can't think about that now. The people still need saving, and we're the ones who must do it. No matter what we are afraid of. No matter what we have or don't have."

Peter kicked the ground. "Which way do we go?"

Harbor pointed across the field. "Stay low. I'll show you the way."

They moved silently and swiftly. Three waspgulls circled overhead. Before long, Opal Pearl's cottage appeared.

All was quiet. Still. Harbor had always thought that Opal Pearl's cottage buzzed with energy. Now it felt dead. Her stomach dropped. Gently, she pushed open the door.

They were greeted with a horrible yell.

CHAPTER THIRTY-FOUR

Without thinking, Harbor jumped. A sword passed under her feet. After she landed, she dove at the attacker. They rolled together on the ground. Harbor landed on top. The attacker yelled so loudly Harbor didn't recognize her at first.

"Brigid?"

The body beneath her stopped moving.

"Harbor, it's you!"

Harbor rolled aside and Brigid sat up. At once, Brigid wrapped Harbor in her arms. "It's terrible, Harbor. The Frost, it's got them all. Took them. Turned them. They are there but not themselves. Except your aunts. Your aunts and your mother they have caged up. Like doves."

"Hush," Harbor told her friend. "You're not making any sense."

"Go and see for yourself," Brigid said. Tears washed down her face. Harbor had never seen Brigid cry.

Peter and Anna stood in the doorway watching this strange reunion. "This is my friend," Harbor said as she got to her feet. "Brigid. She's a soldier in the royal guard."

"Pleased to meet you," Anna said.

Brigid sniffed. "Nice to meet you, too."

"This is Anna. Peter's sister."

"Another hero?"

"I'm no hero," Peter said.

"How are you here, Brigid?" Harbor asked. "How did you get away?"

"Amethyst," Brigid said. She remembered herself and stood, back straight. "She touched me, you know. She made me look like them. It nearly drained all her energy to change my skin, but she did it. 'Run,' she told me. 'Run and find Harbor.' I ran, but I couldn't find you. Not anywhere."

"I found you," Harbor said. She put one hand on each of Brigid's shoulders. "You did your duty, Brigid."

Brigid sniffed again. "It wasn't like I thought at all, Harbor. War, battle, none of it was like I thought. It was messy and terrifying, and I felt *scared*. Scared as a lamb."

Harbor pulled Brigid in tight. They hugged for a long time.

Peter watched them. He felt the same way. His video games and Dungeons & Dragons, they weren't wars. They were fantasies. They were games. This was real.

"Ida's gone," Brigid whispered. "She's one of them." Her body slumped against Harbor's. "I couldn't save her. I watched her go. Watched her turn. It really is like frost. It covered her, slow and cracking. The last thing to go was her eyes. She watched me the whole time. Then the light flashed out of them." Brigid breathed in. "No, that's not right. There was a light there. A sparkle. But it was icy. Then she went for me. I sprinted away. That's when I found Amethyst and she hid me."

Harbor guided Brigid to a chair and brought her a glass of water. Anna looked around the cottage while Peter stood in the corner.

Harbor went outside with Anna behind her. Harbor had taken a small telescope from Opal Pearl's table, and she held it to her eye.

The fort itself was no longer gray granite, but white as limestone. The ground, too. Shapes moved around like bees over a hive. Worst of all were the five hanging cages. They were small, not high enough for anyone to stand, and hung out over the water. In each one, her mother and her aunts, separated. Harbor must have gasped because Anna said, "What is it? Let me see."

Harbor handed Anna the telescope. She did not want to see anymore. But why were they not using their magic? They were close enough together to do something. To change things. Unless they could not.

"Is that The Frost?" Anna asked.

Harbor told her it was.

"I can see why you're so scared. They're creepy." Anna lowered the telescope. "But we'll figure out how to beat them, right?"

Harbor didn't want to lie to Anna, but there was so much hope in her eyes. Harbor could tell it was a precarious hope. She didn't want to shatter it. "We will certainly try," she said.

That was all they could do.

ререр

Harbor made sure Brigid ate and then put her to bed. Anna curled up on the couch and fell asleep almost immediately as well, but neither Peter nor Harbor could lie down. They sat together in the small living area of Opal Pearl's cottage. Harbor's mind raced. They had completed stage one and found their way back to the other side of the island. Now they needed to defeat The Frost and save her family. Unfortunately, they were no closer to knowing how to do that.

A chill came over the island. Peter said he would build a fire. "I used to be a Boy Scout," he said.

"What's that?"

"It's like a club. You learn about outdoors stuff. It was fun, I guess."

Within minutes Peter had a fire blazing. They pulled the armchairs close to the fireplace and let the warmth flow over them. Harbor liked the way the flames danced, orange and red. Peter settled down into his chair with a groan. "I'm sore," he said. "I never really thought about that aspect of it while I was playing my games. One of my friends used to say that war was like a live-action first-person shooter, but in video games, you don't get sore." He sniffed his armpit. "You don't get scrapes, and your hands don't get blisters. You don't smell terrible. Nothing smells as bad as terror sweat."

Harbor sniffed her own armpit and wrinkled up her nose. She *did* smell terrible.

"Anyway, thanks for today," he said. "For helping me on the cliff."

"You're welcome," she said.

"When you touched my arm—I can't explain it. I just felt braver."

Harbor's brain spun. *She* had no magic. She couldn't have passed the bravery to him. Yet that was exactly what it had felt like: like she had pulled it out of herself and passed it on to Peter. How could that possibly be?

Peter leaned forward and poked the fire. "I thought I was going to have a panic attack right there on the ledge, and then I'd be stuck until my arms gave out. I tried to do my breathing, but I couldn't get my body to listen." He shook his head. "Sometimes my brain just won't shut off like that. Plus, I'm really afraid of heights. I don't know why. Maybe it started at that rock gym."

"What *is* a rock gym?" Harbor asked.

"It's like a place where you can go rock climbing?" Peter tried to explain. "There are rocks—well, I guess they are fake rocks. There are ropes and handholds, and you climb the rocks."

"For fun?" Harbor asked.

"It's supposed to be."

"Do the rocks lead anywhere?"

"Just up," he said. "You ring a bell at the top."

"Hm." The Somewhere Else was a strange place.

"Anyway, my dad, he loves heights. Like, for his birthday, he jumped out of a plane."

The light from the fire danced on Peter's face. His mouth turned down, and the dark circle under his eye seemed to deepen. "You used to be happier," she told him.

"Things happened," he said. Then, without even really meaning to, Peter let everything spill out of him. It came so fast, and there was so much anger and sadness in his voice that Harbor had a hard time keeping up. "A lot of it was Cam, I guess. But sometimes it feels like—I don't know. When I first met you, I knew him. He was kind of my friend. We were all kind of friends back then. But then in fourth grade, it changed. I don't know why. He was just—he made fun of me all the time. The clothes I wore. The books I read. My size. The way I threw a baseball. There wasn't anything that I did that he couldn't make fun of. He would do things like trip me or throw a basketball at my head. Mr. Woodson saw him do that, and he got detention, but that just made it worse. My dad said to just punch him. 'Just deck him one good time, and he'll leave you alone.' But I don't like hitting. I don't like fights. I really don't like blood."

An image of The Frost soldier bloody on the ground snapped into Harbor's head. She could see the girl, the smear of blood on her uniform. Harbor could smell it, too, more acrid than the smoke of the fire. She squeezed her eyes shut.

"You okay?"

"I don't like blood either," she said.

Peter nodded. "I once got a bloody nose, and when I saw my own blood, I passed out. How was I supposed to hit Cam? But if I couldn't hit him, how could I be the hero you said I was? Of course, it turns out that wasn't true. But I didn't know that then. When I first saw that door and crawled through, it was like my own Narnia. But better. And I thought, 'Okay. Okay, maybe I'm not a loser.' But my dad kept telling me to toughen up and get my head out of the clouds. And I figured, I'm never going to beat Cam in a fight. But I am smarter than him. I could fight him with words. So, I said something I shouldn't have. I didn't mumble it. I said it right to his face."

Harbor motioned toward his black eye. "I guess your plan didn't work?"

Peter laughed bitterly. "He pounded me. He turned around and punched me in the face, and when I fell, he jumped on me and kept hitting my stomach until I puked, and then he punched me once more just for good measure. I came home, suspended, and my dad said, 'Never start a fight you can't finish.' Like it was all my fault."

There were tears streaming down Peter's face now. He wiped at them with his fist. "And here, this place where I'm supposed to be the hero, you have to save me. So even here, even here . . ." His voice trailed off into a sob.

"What do you think a hero is?" Harbor asked.

"A hero saves people. A hero is the star of the story."

Harbor thought about that. She supposed that was what

she'd always thought, too. Like her father: big, bold, brave, and heroic. But maybe her mother, who had left her lands, the world she had known and loved, was a hero, too. Maybe it meant more than saving people. "I think a hero does what's right, even when it's hard. I think a hero makes sacrifices."

Peter sniffed.

"Maybe making fun of Cam didn't feel good and didn't fix things, because you were doing the wrong thing or the easy thing."

"It wasn't easy—"

"Easier than your dad being disappointed in you," Harbor said.

Peter frowned. He picked up the poker and jabbed at the logs in the fire. They broke apart into glowing embers. "It's not so easy to know what's right and what's wrong."

He kept crying. Harbor didn't know what to do or what to say. She had never had a friend confess all their feelings to her at once. She wasn't sure if she'd ever even truly had a friend. Brigid was the closest, or maybe Frank. But they kept their thoughts to themselves, for the most part.

Harbor looked at her hands in her lap. She looked at Peter. Then she reached across the space between the chairs. It wasn't a very big space. She placed her hand on top of his. She didn't know what to say to make him feel better. Maybe there was nothing to say. Maybe this would have to be enough.

PART FIVE

CHAPTER THIRTY-FIVE

In the morning, Brigid was more herself. She was outside doing her calisthenics before sunup. When Harbor came down, the sky was red and so was Brigid's face. "I'm ready to fight them," she said.

"There is no them," Harbor said. "The Frost is us. Our people. Or other people who have families and friends." She sat on Opal Pearl's stoop next to the watermelon that never grew. "I killed one. It thanked me."

Brigid stopped her movements.

"They're still in there," Harbor said. "We can't fight them." She chewed on her bottom lip. "There's something else I need to tell you."

"Go on," Brigid said.

Harbor told her about Micah. She told her about meeting her in the woods and then again on the beach. She told her about the dream she and Peter had shared.

"Micah?" Brigid demanded. "You want me to trust Micah of all people?"

"Her story makes sense."

"Her story casts your father as a villain."

"Not a villain exactly—"

"The people of Benspeir are not greedy. They never would have done those things. It was a trick! Some of her evil magic, to be sure."

Peter opened the door and stepped outside. He wiped the sleep from his eyes. "Morning," he said. "It's so pretty here it's hard to believe anything's wrong."

"Everything is wrong," Brigid said. She shook her arms as if she was shaking off the damp. "So how do you propose we rescue our people from whatever has them trapped?"

"I've been thinking about that," Peter said. "Remember how I talked about zombies and vampires? Well, with zombies, it's like game over. You're a zombie and that's that. No turning back. You're one of the undead, and then you're just, well, dead."

"Sounds good to me," Brigid said.

Peter went on, "With vampires, if you kill the head vampire, some legends say that all their minions or sub-vampires or whatever go back to being humans. Then there's like mind control movies. Like everyone's brain gets taken over by some central being that controls them all."

"Can you undo that?" Harbor asked.

"Well in the movies they can. It all depends on the internal mythology of the movie, you know. With the Borg in Star Trek, the nanoprobes and other technology can be removed, but it's still a long way back to humanity. But that's super techy, so of course that doesn't apply here."

Brigid stabbed her sword into the grass. "All this talking isn't saving anybody."

"Do you want Ida back?" Harbor demanded.

The color in Brigid's cheeks flared. "Of course I do."

"Peter has knowledge. He may be the only one who can figure out how to get our people back. So, if he needs a little time to work it out, he gets a little time."

Peter started pacing. "Let's start with what we know. When you, um, shot your arrow at The Frost soldier, it turned human again."

"For barely a breath," Harbor said.

"But that means whatever it is they're doing to people, it isn't permanent."

For the first time in days, a spark of hope lit in Harbor. A tiny little flame deep in her chest; it wanted to grow. "And we know it was stopped before," she said.

"How?" Brigid asked.

"The people from the Soth lands were able to subdue it somehow. Then magical women from Lapistyr took it from the people and sent it back to the earth," Harbor said. "Back where it belongs."

"We don't have time to call for the people of the Soth lands," Brigid said.

"But we can find out what they did!" Harbor said. "Come on, we need to go to the library!"

"The library?" Brigid shook her head. "Not possible. It's too close to the fort. Too close to The Frost."

"I'm sure Amethyst has books about this history. If we can read about what they did way back then, we can do it now."

Brigid took a deep breath. "We're going to need a distraction."

Harbor smiled. "I know just the thing."

∼∼∼∼

"You sure you don't have any of Amethyst's magic?" Brigid asked her.

To be able to change their appearance would have been a great help. Instead, they would have to make disguises. Fortunately, Opal Pearl's studio was the perfect place to do so. Brigid found a bolt of white fabric and cut makeshift tunics for them. Clay powder worked to blanch their faces. When they were done, they looked like ghosts.

"Are you sure the little one should go?" Brigid asked Peter. Anna in her disguise looked like a child playing dress-up, and there was no place for games in a time like this.

"I can't leave her alone," Peter said. "Not in such a dangerous place."

"I'm sorry," Harbor said.

"You keep saying that, but you're not," Peter said. He didn't sound angry, but Harbor rocked back all the same. She *was* sorry. She had never meant to put Peter and his sister into this dangerous situation. She would undo it if she could. "But you called me on purpose."

"Yes, but—"

He shook his head, his face tight. "I liked that idea. I liked that I was needed somewhere. I guess I just didn't realize quite what the battle would be. I thought it would be more like a video game."

"A what?"

"Never mind," he said. "I guess, if I'm being honest, I didn't think that I would really be hurt. I guess that's why I thought it was okay to bring Anna. I mean, I figured you were lonely again and she would get to see the island." He rubbed his eyes. "I'm too tired to think, but what I guess I mean is, you needed a hero, so you called me. I'm not mad about that, but I think you did know the danger."

"I suppose you're right," Harbor admitted.

"And I should have," he said. "To me this was a fantasy world, but for you it was real. That meant the war was real and you needed a real hero. I thought it would be like playing soldier in my backyard. I should have known better."

Brigid cleared her throat. "I thought we were done with yammering," she said. "Let's go."

Harbor and Peter exchanged one last look. This wasn't what either of them had wanted or expected, but now that they were in it, they had no other choice but to go through with their thin plan.

ᴥᴥᴥ

Six small fire circles, each filled with a different color of deatree leaves, led from the bend in the path below Harbor's house to the rocks. Peter had built the fire circles of stones as they crept along the path. The circles, he said, should keep the fire from spreading.

"They won't all leave the fort," Brigid told them. "But wait until there are few left. Do you have your bow?"

"I won't shoot them," Harbor said.

"Sometimes, we have no choice," Brigid said. She handed Harbor a small dagger. "If needs be, you must save yourself."

Harbor, Peter, and Anna crept through the garden behind the hotel. The windows had all been smashed. The grounds around it had turned white. What was left of the topiaries, though, gave them enough shelter to make it to Shady Lane where they hid in the Templetons' house and waited for the smoke.

Harbor used Opal Pearl's small telescope to watch the fort. She saw her mother crouched in her cage. Coralie's red hair was a bird's nest of tangles, her face stained. Harbor still could not understand why her mother had lied to her all those years. Anger burned, but also worry. She had to save her mother. They could sort everything out once they were all safe.

"There," Peter said. "She's lit the red one." Crimson smoke from red deatree leaves drifted into the sky.

It took a moment for The Frost to notice. They stopped their movement and turned their heads in the direction of the smoke. When the orange leaves were lit, they looked at one another. When the yellow smoke hit the sky, they began to move. With the green, more than half The Frost left the fort. Blue sent still more soldiers in the direction of the smoke.

Harbor trained her telescope on Ruby. Ruby waved back.

Purple smoke twisted into the sky. It was time.

They ran as fast as they could down Shady Lane toward the library. They scurried behind the last house. Checked the road for soldiers. None. They ran on, heading for the front steps of the library. At the last moment, she realized her mistake. Amethyst had bolted the doors.

She swerved to the left and gestured for the others to follow. Fists pumping, she ran around the back.

The front of the library was solid with its stone steps and heavy wooden door, but the back was made of glass. Windows reached nearly from the ground to the ceiling, each made up of several good-sized panes.

She sat on her bottom and kicked the glass. The window cracked but did not break.

Peter sat beside her. "On three," he whispered. "One, two, three!"

They kicked together. The glass shattered.

Harbor took the scarf from around her face and wrapped it around her arm and smashed away the glass.

She eased herself in, careful of shards, and dropped to the floor.

The library was dark. Shadows loomed. She helped Anna, and then Peter followed.

The circulation desk was empty.

The tables, too.

The silence was eerie. No shrift as the page of a book turned. No happy whisper from Amethyst. No sniffling or coughing. Silence.

CHAPTER THIRTY-SIX

History books were stacked on the floor around Harbor, Peter, and Anna. "None of them? None have the history of Benspeir?" Harbor demanded.

She tried to remember when she had asked Amethyst about her father's kingdom; where had she gone to look for a book? Had she even gone at all?

She played with her necklace charms: the sand, the shell, the lens. Sapphire had said that lenses showed things in new ways. Maybe . . . ?

"Maybe it's not in history," Peter said. "Maybe it's in myths and legends."

"But it's true," Harbor said.

"But they kept it hidden, didn't they?" Peter asked. "My history teacher said that we can look at myths and legends and odes and stuff and get hints about what life was like and what they valued. Maybe we can get enough of a hint from those books."

"We don't have time for that," Harbor said.

Anna rubbed her eyes and smeared her white makeup. Harbor had to act quickly. They wouldn't be safe here for much longer.

She rubbed her thumb on her shell, and then, because she had no other ideas, she held the lens Sapphire had given her to her eye. A glow appeared in the corner of her eye. Harbor swiveled her head. The light was coming from The Locked Room. When she moved the lens, the light went away.

"I think I know where it is," Harbor said and led them toward the room.

Curious as Harbor was, Amethyst had done such a good job of making The Locked Room sound boring that Harbor had never wanted to go in. It was more of a cage than a room with the books locked in and the people locked out. The lock was part of the door, an elaborately carved circle with the keyhole at the center.

"Do you know where the key is?" Peter asked.

Harbor thought of the disaster that was Amethyst's room. It could be anywhere.

"Maybe I can fit through the bars," Anna said. She reached an arm and leg through, but her head would not fit.

"Let me try," Peter said. "Give me that clip from your hair."

Harbor gave him Amethyst's hair clip. He bent the fastener. "Hey!" she protested.

Peter turned to his sister. "You can never, ever tell Mom and Dad that I did this."

Before she could respond, Peter turned back to the lock. He fiddled and fidgeted with the hair clip, and then *pop* the lock unlatched.

"Where did you learn to do that?" Anna asked.

"YouTube," Peter replied. "And like I said, don't tell."

Harbor threw open the door. "I'll go in. You keep watch." She went right to the history section. There were tomes and tomes on the history of Lapistyr but only one about Benspeir. Harbor recognized it. Amethyst had shown it to her one day. She'd been trying to tell Harbor about her family's past, but Harbor hadn't picked up on the message.

She flipped through the book. The story she wanted was right near the beginning.

"Harbor!" Anna cried. "They're coming back!"

Harbor tucked the book under her arm. Back out through the window, they went, then up the open field behind the library. They ran straight into the woods.

ᔪᔪᔪ

Under a pink and gray sky, a battle raged at the foot of a mountain. The Frost, all in white, powered over the soldiers of the Soth lands.

Harbor turned the page. Now the Soth soldiers surrounded The Frost. A small figure, dressed in red and blue, stood facing The Frost. In the next image, the bodies of The Frost were on the ground. Specks of dust rose out of them. Brave soldiers from all over the realm stood around the bodies. They held their shields toward the hole in the ground, ready to fight again. A single waspgull perched in the tree, out of the rain. Near the center of the illustration were the magical women of Lapistyr.

"This is it," Harbor said and pushed the book toward the others. They had made their way back to the forest encampment. There wasn't much left of it. They had found Brigid in one of the last remaining structures, and now they all looked at the book.

"What are they doing?" Brigid asked. "Are they pushing it in? How did they get it out of the people?"

"The pictures do seem to leave out some key details," Peter said.

"That soldier is awfully small," Anna said, pointing at a figure very close to the hole.

Harbor flipped back and read as quickly as she could.

"What's it say?" Peter demanded.

"It says that The Frost never sleep, but that only when they sleep can the curse be lifted."

"Well, that's a real help. Did it say how they got them to sleep?"

"There's not very much about that. It says that a shepherd boy knew how to make them sleep. That's all. Then they led it to the hole," Harbor explained.

"Led it?" Peter asked.

"With magic words. Magic is one of The Frost's weaknesses."

"This whole island is surrounded by magic," Brigid said. "Your aunts protected us with it."

"Maybe it's not the right kind of spell," Harbor said. "It says that magic can compel The Frost, but maybe you need to tell it what to do, not just to not come." She paused. "If we can get The Frost to sleep, we can get the spell off our people. Then my mother and aunts can compel it into the ground."

"So, all we have to do is get The Frost to sleep and get your mom and aunts out of those cages. Easy peasy," Peter said.

"Really?" Brigid asked. "How do you suggest we do it?"

"I was being sarcastic."

"Does anyone have any useful ideas?" Brigid asked.

Harbor looked at the darkening sky. She saw rain in the distance. "Actually, I do. But we'd better hurry."

CHAPTER THIRTY-SEVEN

Are you sure your aunt left this killer root in her cottage?" Peter asked.

"No," Harbor admitted. They had made their way along the forest paths in the direction of Ruby's cottage.

Harbor hoped that the root wasn't in Ruby's satchel, which was, presumably, with Ruby. She hoped that Ruby had tucked it away. Hidden. She had held up the lens from Sapphire, and the forest had glowed, but that didn't necessarily mean that the root was in the forest. Maybe there was something else in the forest they were meant to find. Maybe the lens just lit things up for no reason at all. The fact was, even with all their gifts, her aunts had not prepared her for this.

Brigid climbed a tree and peered in all directions, then, just as quickly, climbed down. "It looks clear," she said. "Stay quiet."

Anna slipped her hand into Peter's.

The path to Ruby's cottage was well worn. The trees arched over it and shook their leaves at the group that walked below.

"I don't think I like these woods," Anna said.

"Hush," Brigid told her. "The woods don't like that kind of talk."

Anna looked over her shoulder at Harbor.

"Ruby told me that plants can talk to each other through their roots, but I don't think they can understand humans," Harbor said.

"Why would they want to?" Peter asked.

They walked on until Ruby's cottage came into view. It sat bathed in sun in the middle of the clearing. It was squat and round with a thatched roof and built of round stones that swirled together rubies and white quartz. The windows were made of multicolored glass.

Anna froze. Harbor nearly ran into her. "Are you okay?" Harbor asked.

"I'll wait outside," she said.

"What's wrong?" Brigid asked.

Anna shook her head, but Peter said, "The cottage looks like it's made of candy."

Harbor had never thought that, but she supposed it could be considered a little candy-like.

"In our world, there's a story about a witch who tempts children and then fattens them up and eats them," Peter explained.

"Your world has a lot of strange stories!" Harbor said. She squatted in front of Anna. "My aunt would never, ever, eat a child. She's the sweetest magic woman you would ever meet."

"Then why'd she keep that root that can kill you?" Anna asked.

"She just . . . did," Harbor said. She didn't have an explanation, and the secrecy had bothered her, too.

"But the queen told her not to," Anna pressed. "She defied her queen."

"It's a good thing she did," Brigid said.

It was another mystery Harbor didn't have the answer to. So many secrets! She hoped that Amethyst had been right: that Ruby just couldn't bear to see any living thing destroyed. "They're sisters. It's different. Ruby would never—" But Harbor thought of what the women had told her, and what they had not. She thought of the slippery way Ruby had hidden the root in her bag. She thought of Micah, the supposed villain who seemed to be the only one willing to tell her the truth.

But it was Ruby! There was no one kinder than Ruby. She tended to seals in the ocean for goodness' sakes!

"You all need to stop your fussing," Brigid told them. "We need to get in there and find the root and go."

"Come on, Anna," Peter prodded.

Anna's feet were glued to the ground.

Ruby was the nicest, Harbor conceded, but there were other times when she had defied orders. So had Amethyst, for that matter. They'd told her things they weren't meant to. They'd strayed, as Leo had put it. But did that make them the good ones or the bad ones? *The good ones or the bad ones?* She chided herself in her own head. These were her aunts and her mother!

"Honestly, child, I understand that a war is no place for a little girl," Brigid said to Anna, "but we simply can't hesitate any longer. We simply must—"

"Look out!" Peter cried.

Ada Flynn raced from the woods

Or, the body of the person who used to be Ada Flynn did.

Ada's once dark hair was now white as snow, her skin like ice on a river. She spoke not a word but reached for a knife at her waist.

Ada Flynn had never carried a knife.

"Harbor!" Brigid cried. She leapt forward and pushed the Once-Ada to the ground. In a swift move, Brigid pulled her sword from her scabbard.

"Wait!" Harbor yelled.

Brigid froze. Her blade pushed against the creature's chest.

"That's Ada," Harbor said. "Can't you see?"

Brigid shook her head. "It isn't Ada anymore."

"But it could be again. Right, Peter?"

"What?" Peter said. He pushed Anna behind him.

"You said they could go back! Like vampires!"

"I mean, it's a working theory—"

Harbor turned her attention back to Brigid. "You can't kill her."

Brigid pushed her blade a little farther. A spot of black blood appeared. The Once-Ada gasped. For a second, her eyes flickered back to normal. Then she raged, reaching for the blade.

"She means to kill us," Brigid growled, fighting off the attacks.

She stumbled back, and the Once-Ada scrambled to her feet. Her knife was lost, but still she rushed at Brigid. She was fast and nimble. Brigid was pushed back against a tree.

Harbor rushed forward. She shoved Once-Ada to the ground. Brigid was on her at once, sword drawn.

"No," Harbor said firmly. "I order you to let her live."

"Order?" Brigid asked.

"Find some rope," she said to Peter. "We'll tie her up."

Brigid stood. "Very well," she said. "If that is your order, *I* will not defy it." She stared meaningfully at the cottage.

Peter and Harbor tied Once-Ada up with rope from Ruby's greenhouse while Brigid stood over their captive, sword still drawn. "Find it quick so we can be on our way," Brigid told them, still smarting from being given orders by children.

Fortunately, Ruby was well organized. Harbor threw open the cupboard at the G section and immediately found the gullsbane. Just above it was echinacea, so she grabbed some of that, too.

"Hurry," Peter said. He stared out the window into the woods.

"One more thing," Harbor said. Harbor did not have Ruby's magic, but she had learned enough. Echinacea helped with sickness. A salve of marshroot could help heal a wound. She knew where Ruby kept that as well. She found one of Ruby's extra satchels and filled it with herbs, tinctures, and salves her people might need once they were freed.

Brigid stepped inside. "Are you nearly ready?"

Harbor took a book down from the shelf, one she had seen Ruby consult hundreds of times: *Plants, Herbs, Flowers, and the Natural Magic Therein.* "Now I am."

Outside the window, Once-Ada writhed against the ground. She had dug holes with her feet. Foam dripped from her mouth. They could hear her screams and moans.

"Should we give her some?" Harbor asked. "If she were sleeping, she might not be so miserable."

"It would give us a chance to test our plan," Brigid said.

"Testing on a person? I don't know about that," Peter said.

"She's not a person right now," Brigid told him.

Harbor could see what Peter meant. If they were wrong, they might kill Once-Ada and the true Ada along with her. Harbor wasn't sure she could bear to have that on her conscience. But if they did nothing, they all would die. "We must," she said.

While Brigid returned outside to keep watch, Harbor opened Ruby's book.

"I can help," Anna said.

"No! It's too dangerous," Peter said. He turned to Harbor. "How much do we need to put them all to sleep?"

"Well," Harbor began. "Ruby wasn't entirely precise. She said a drop would put someone to sleep. She said too much would kill them. So, for all those people, we need somewhere between a drop and too much."

"Perfect," Peter muttered.

"The book says to squeeze the juice from the root." Using tweezers from Ruby's workbench, Harbor dropped the gullsbane root into Ruby's mortar and pestle.

"I really don't know about this, Harbor," Peter said. "What if we fail? What if we mess this whole thing up? What if my sister and I are stuck here forever?"

Harbor used the pestle to push hard against the purple root, releasing its juices. "There are worse places to be stuck than Small Island."

"Maybe we should think some more," Peter said. "We really shouldn't be making decisions because of the books I read or the movies I watch. They aren't real. There's no such thing as vampires or zombies."

"In your world," Harbor said. Her fingers were white around the pestle as if she were squeezing ever drop of her anger into the root.

"They're just stories, Harbor; somebody made them up."

"You said I was a story in your world, too," Harbor said. "You said it was a story everyone knew, the cursed princess who falls asleep. And I'm real as real."

Peter frowned. "It's not exactly the same story. You didn't sleep for a hundred years."

Anna rolled her eyes. "It's close enough."

"Fine!" Peter said, exasperated. "But don't blame me if it all goes wrong."

Harbor looked at the liquid she had squeezed from the root. There was hardly any, maybe a teaspoon at most. She found one of Ruby's vials and carefully poured it in.

"Really, Harbor, are you sure about this?" Peter asked. His voice was softer now.

Harbor thought of her father who was so sure in everything he did. Every word, every step, every choice. Sapphire, too. Her words rang out with a finality that no one dared challenge. Even her mother, in her quiet way, had a surety about her. Did this come with being an adult?

Harbor wasn't sure if this was the right choice. She wasn't sure who to trust anymore. Maybe, that was just how it was. Maybe sometimes you knew what you had to do, like how Harbor knew she could not let Brigid kill Ada. Other times, you weren't sure. Either way, sometimes you had to make a decision and go with it. Perhaps her father's certainty was real, or perhaps it was another mask. Perhaps he was sometimes as confused as she was now.

"No," she said. "I'm not sure. But we have to make a choice and this is the one I'm making."

Harbor turned once again to the book. For a sleeping potion, the root needed to be ground and then mixed with water. Caution had to be taken as stray drops of root juice could get on the preparer's fingers and lead to unwanted consequences.

"Unwanted consequences like death," said Peter, who was reading over her shoulder.

Once it was in the form of a tea, it was almost impossible to drink to the point of death, although there was a recorded case of a man who drank so much of a strong brew that he slept for one hundred years.

From Ruby's sink, she filled a glass of water. She poured the water into the mortar bowl, then poured it all back into the glass. She hoped there was enough gullsbane root. She hoped there was not too much.

"You know the discovery of penicillin was accidental," Peter said. "Alexander Fleming came back to his lab after a holiday, and he was checking on his little strep samples, and one had some mold in it, and the strep was gone, and he realized that there was something in the mold that killed the bacteria."

"Encyclopedia mouth," Anna said.

Peter rubbed his head hard. "I don't want to kill anybody."

"You aren't going to," Harbor said. She placed Ruby's satchel over her shoulder, took the water, and went outside.

Once-Ada writhed in her ropes.

"She's not getting any happier," Brigid said.

Harbor watched the face of her neighbor contort in anger. Once-Ada sneered and spit at Harbor. "You need to sleep,"

Harbor said. She knew she couldn't convince Once-Ada to drink. "Hold her mouth," Harbor said to Brigid.

Brigid crouched behind Once-Ada. She wrapped one arm around Once-Ada's head and used her other hand to squeeze open her mouth. The Frost creature squirmed, but still made no sound. Harbor poured the drink down Once-Ada's throat. The creature coughed and sputtered. So much of the brew lost! But then, slowly, the body stilled.

"Is she dying?" Anna asked.

"Sleeping," Brigid said. She checked the pulse to confirm.

"Wait," Harbor said. She knew a thing about sleep and death and fear. They watched as the body stilled and its breath came in a slow, rhythmic motion. "Sleep well, Ada. We will return for you."

The gazes of the others turned from Once-Ada to Harbor. She stood. "It's time," she said. "It's time to end this."

CHAPTER THIRTY-EIGHT

The clouds mounted in the sky behind the fort and the cages.

"Never would I have thought I'd see this day. The magic women of Lapistyr all caged up," Brigid said.

Their plan was to get The Frost soldiers to consume the gullsbane. Then her aunts could take the magic off them. It was, Harbor admitted, not the firmest of plans. First, there was the issue of getting The Frost to consume the gullsbane. Next, there was the matter of getting her mother and aunts free from their cages. Harbor could only think of one step at a time. First, the gullsbane.

"What if we smoked it to them?" Anna said.

"They have to eat it or drink it; that's what the book says," Peter reminded her.

Brigid pointed toward the fort. "Look: they're eating. They're drinking. We just drop it in the water cisterns."

"Just drop it in?" Peter said. "Are you going to run in there and drop it?"

"I could," Brigid said. "I'd sacrifice myself if that's what it took."

"No one's sacrificing themselves," Harbor said, though, in truth, she was willing to give up her own life if that was what it took to save the others.

"Cinderella would have the birds bring it," Anna said.

"I thought it was mice that helped her," Peter said.

"That was in the movie. In the Grimm story, it was birds. When her evil stepmother told her to separate the peas, the birds came and helped. At the end, they pecked out her stepsisters' eyeballs."

"How gruesome!" Harbor exclaimed.

"They were truly terrible stepsisters," Anna told her.

"Well, we can't ask the birds to do it," Harbor said. "It's a danger to them as well."

"But we could make it fly," Brigid said. A smile spread over her face, and she pulled an arrow from her quiver. The point glinted.

"Are you actually considering shooting it in like some kind of Hawkeye trick arrow thing?" Peter asked.

"Who is Hawkeye?" Brigid replied.

"Well, there's more than one. It's kind of complicated. Anyway, is that your plan? To attach the root to the arrow and shoot it in?"

"It's not a terrible plan," Brigid said. "The water is right in the sun. It would steep like tea."

"All of The Frost would have to drink it," Harbor said. "It's risky."

They all looked down at the fort, at the white creatures that moved about it like bees on a hive.

"Two cisterns, two shots," Brigid said. "I hope you have your bow."

෬෬෬

The sun glinted off the water. It burned Harbor's eyes. Everything between her and the ocean looked hazy as if reflected in a water-covered mirror.

"I can't," Harbor said. She held her bow by her side. It had been dinged up in all their travels. That didn't bother her. What bothered her was that she had used it to kill someone. The one time she hit her target it was to take a life.

"You have to," Brigid said. "There are two cisterns. We can't hit them separately. It will draw too much notice."

The large cisterns were each on the outside wall of the fort. The water flowed into the fort through a series of pipes designed by Archie Murphy and crafted to his precise specifications.

"You can do it," Anna said. "I believe in you!"

"We've practiced this," Brigid said.

"Yeah, and I always miss."

"Not always," Brigid said. "Not this time." She notched an arrow into her bow. "My first shot will distract them. Then we fire into the cisterns."

Brigid's arrow was covered in feathers of all different birds. They'd found them in Opal Pearl's studio, and Anna had worked to make the arrow look like a majestic bird. They hoped it would distract The Frost long enough for them to shoot their pouches of gullsbane into the cisterns.

Then they would hide. The shakiest part of their plan was that it relied on The Frost drinking. None of them were sure how long it would take for each of them to drink, and, if some of The Frost started falling asleep, would those left realize what had gone wrong? It was a risk they had to take. After all, they had no other plan.

"I am going to shoot the bird arrow, and then we are going to shoot together," Brigid said, her voice slow and clam. "You are going to make this shot."

"I can't," Harbor said again.

Peter came and stood beside her. "If I could give you back that drop of bravery, I would."

"Thanks," Harbor said with a sniff.

"I wish I knew how to shoot a bow and arrow," he said. "I think I focused my training on the wrong things. Strategy and spycraft weren't exactly needed here."

"You knew how to pick the lock," Harbor said. "You were the one who realized we could save our people. That's why you're the hero."

"Yeah, about that," he said. "We both know I'm not the hero."

"Don't say that," she said. "Don't lose confidence now. Perhaps you aren't a full-grown man as I was hoping, but—"

"No—"

281

"I'm sorry I chided you for your lack of preparation when you first arrived, but, truly, your knowledge is what's going to save us."

Brigid paced beside them. "We're running out of time."

Peter ignored her and kept talking to Harbor. "I was thinking about the story those people told, about you washing up here."

"I don't want to talk about that right now," she said.

"We have to," he said, his voice firmer than it ever had been before. "Anna was right. You could be from anywhere. You could be from any land or any realm. That means *you* are from far away, too."

Harbor shook her head, but something was starting to click in her brain. "No," she said. "I pricked my finger, and then you came from far away. A stranger from far away. That makes you the hero."

"That was your assumption, and it was a logical one. But there is such a thing as coincidence. Or unintended consequences." He stepped closer to her. "You're from here and not from here. You're strange and new. One hundred percent. You are like nothing this world has ever seen." He reached out and put his hands on her shoulder. "You fell asleep," he said, "and arose a hero. You are the hero, Harbor. You always have been."

Waspgulls drew figure eights in the sky while Harbor's thoughts spun.

"I don't have any magic," she said.

"Neither do I, but that didn't stop you from thinking I could be the hero."

Brigid had stopped her pacing. "I'll be a crab in a cage! I can't believe I never saw it before now. It all makes perfect sense."

"It would have been nice to be the hero," Peter said. "But, honestly, it's a lot of pressure, and in this scenario, I get to be the sidekick. That's a role I'm more comfortable with anyway. I get all the zingers."

Anna slipped her hand into Harbor's. "I think you're pretty magical," she said.

Peter went on, "I knew for sure earlier when you made the choice about Ada. You said you weren't sure if you were right, but you had to make a choice. That's what a hero does."

"And a leader, too," Brigid added.

"Micah said you were the only one who could solve this problem. I think it's because you're like this place. You're in between. All of it adds up."

Micah had told her it was her choice. That it was up to her.

Me? A hero? She repeated it over and over in her head until it wasn't a question anymore.

It was truth.

Me. A hero.

CHAPTER THIRTY-NINE

From where they stood on the hillside, the sun glinted off the ocean while far off, the clouds were gathering in the sky.

"This has been a stunning revelation," Brigid said. "But we still have a rescue to mount. You're the hero, Harbor. You need to shoot the arrow."

Her feelings were still a jumble, but Harbor knew one devastating thing for certain. "I'm a terrible shot," she said. "I need better sight. If I miss—"

"Good thing your aunt thought of that," Peter said. He pointed at her marble-shaped lens. She lifted the lens to her eye. Everything sharpened. She could see the line the arrow needed to travel. "Hold this here," she told Peter.

He took the glass from her hand and held it against her eye. "Is that okay?" he asked. "Am I pushing too hard?"

"No, it's just right," she told him. "I can do this."

Brigid gave a sharp nod. "As soon as the root arrows fly, we all run."

"Aye, aye," Anna said.

Brigid shot her first arrow. It flew high above the fort, whistling as it went. The Frost heard the sound and stared at the sky. At once, The Frost began scrambling. A soldier banged the large leather drum.

"Now," Brigid cried.

Together they let their arrows fly. Brigid's went faster, but each met their target. *Splash, splash.*

Through the lens, Harbor saw her mother. Coralie held her fingers to her lips, kissed them, then let the kiss fly to Harbor.

"Run," Brigid urged.

They all ran.

Harbor wished they could make it to the lighthouse. That felt like the safest place, away from the bodies that were and were not her friends and family. She wished they could make it to Ruby's cozy cottage in the woods. Instead, they returned to the library. Harbor led them to Amethyst's rooms. They barricaded the door and took turns watching out the window.

Anna picked up one of Amethyst's silk scarves and wrapped it around her neck. She took a second one and draped it over Harbor's hair, then tied it under her chin. "Now you look like a princess."

"She looks like a granny," Peter said.

Harbor rearranged the scarf over her shoulders. "My aunt Amethyst can change the colors of these. She touches them and makes them the right shade."

Anna's eyes grew wide. "Really? What else can she do?"

"She can change her hair color by touch. Every day she had a different color. She gave me these extra freckles, too," Harbor said, touching her cheek. "She's a Shifter."

"What about your other aunts?"

"Well, Ruby is a Healer and a wonder with plants. She makes regular things like jams and medicines, but she does other stuff, too. I guess you'd call them spells. That's how I knew about the deatree and the gullsbane. But she can make their properties stronger—their energy."

"What about the one who lives up on the hill?"

"Opal Pearl? She's a Protector and puts her magic into her art. The sculptures around the island protect us. Sapphire, she's a Seer. Her magic is about seeing things not just with her eyes but with her mind and her heart. It's like she can see the energy and then know what to do."

"And your mother?"

"Oh, my mother's magic is small."

"Aye!" Brigid cried. "I'll have no such talk about the queen. Your mother has strengths you'll never know."

Harbor shrugged. "At least she has some magic. I don't have any."

"You don't need it," Peter said. "You have your smarts." He pointed out the window. "It's starting."

They all rushed to the window. Sure enough, The Frost were starting to fall asleep.

It was time for phase two of the plan.

CHAPTER FORTY

Harbor could see the rain hitting the water. It would only be a matter of time before the storm was upon them, and that would only make their challenge harder.

Harbor knew it would not be so simple as finding a key on one of The Frost. Still, that was where they started. They walked carefully among the sleeping forms. There was Leo Murphy, his rosy cheeks replaced by ashy white. There was Ida, her regal uniform replaced by the white tunic of The Frost. There was Archie Murphy, no smile on his lips.

"Frank," came a call. The voice was so soft and cracked Harbor hardly recognized it. She looked at the cages. "Frank," said Opal Pearl again in that same unfamiliar voice. She was curled up in her cage, coiled on her side. Would they even have the energy to cast whatever magic they needed to?

Opal Pearl raised a shaking hand and pointed to the wall beneath her. A body sat leaning against it. Frank. His skin was as pale as a fish's belly. His hair, once a shock of deep brown, now fell ghostly and flat against his head. Harbor held her hand to her stomach, sick at the sight of him. This was not her Frank.

The keys were looped in his belt. "I've got them," Harbor called softly.

Brigid was already climbing up the walls.

Harbor crouched down beside Frank. She reached for the keys. Frank let out a long breath. She stumbled back.

Peter came behind her. "You need me to do it?"

She shook her head. She reached out again and placed her fingers on the key ring. She gave a little tug. Nothing.

She took the keys with her other hand, spun them around, looking for a fastener.

Harbor looked back over her shoulder. "I can't get them, I can't—"

Icy fingers gripped her wrist.

She jumped back, crashing into Peter. He caught her.

Frank blinked open his eyes. Before, they were warm brown, but now they were the palest blue.

Harbor pushed Peter back.

"Harbor?" Frank asked. "The hero?"

"Yes," Peter said behind her.

Harbor shook like winter berries. Frank reached down. His movements were slow as if through molasses. He fumbled with the keys. What was he doing? Was he helping or was he going to throw the keys into the ocean?

He unclipped the keys and then held them out to Harbor. "Please," he said. "Save us."

Harbor took the keys from him. "Up here!" Brigid yelled.

Harbor threw the keys to Brigid who caught them easily. Then Harbor fell to her knees next to Frank, but he had fallen asleep again. At that moment, the sky opened and the rain started to fall.

CHAPTER FORTY-ONE

Weakened and rain-drenched, the magical women of Lapistyr looked like the drowned animals on the ship that Mr. Broom had described. The women stood in the center of the fort, surrounded by the bodies of their friends.

"It will be hard to pull it off them," Sapphire said. "Hate, anger, and jealousy are powerful sticky."

"The rain will help," Harbor said.

"It's had so long to grow," Ruby said. "Like roots in soil."

Harbor remembered how Ruby had told her that the roots were how trees spoke to one another, and she wondered if the roots of The Frost were still contacting one another. Who was leading them now that all were asleep?

"Are you well enough?" Coralie asked Sapphire.

Sapphire straightened her crooked spine. "I am well enough to put an end to this, yes. Even if it is the last magic I do." She lifted a set of lenses to her eyes. "The way forward is clear to me."

The women stepped closer together. Harbor had always liked watching them do their magic, but now something stirred in her. Something wasn't right.

The women gripped hands and tilted their heads into the rain. Drops slid off their chins. They began to chant words that Harbor did not know or understand.

Anna, who stood between Peter and Harbor, took each of their hands. "Is it happening?" she asked.

"Yes," Harbor said. Again, her stomach sunk.

"They're getting rid of it," Peter said.

"But where will it go?" Anna asked. The white film was starting to run off the people of Small Island. It streamed in rivulets and gathered in puddles.

"Into the earth, I suppose," Peter sad. "They said they were going to capture it."

The children jumped out of the way of a stream of white.

"Like they did before?" Anna asked.

Yes, Harbor thought. Just like before, they would bury it deep and never talk about it. "Wait!" she cried.

Everyone turned to look at her.

"We have to let it go," Harbor said.

"Let it go?" Peter asked, incredulous.

"There's not time for this," Sapphire said.

"Let her speak," Queen Coralie said. Though Sapphire was the eldest and Coralie the youngest, Sapphire was compelled to listen to her queen. "Go on," Coralie said to Harbor.

"The Frost is the bitter root of us. Our anger and shame and jealousy and all that. Those feelings grow on

291

themselves." She looked over at Peter and his black eye. "When we bury them down, they fester. And then someone can let them out and they're even stronger. But if we let it go, it dissipates."

Peter, at least, understood. "If you trap it again, it's only going to be madder. Like a bear."

"They hid it before," Harbor said. "They hid it, and then they hid their mistakes and didn't talk about any of it, and that was the biggest mistake of all. We need to let it go. Into the sea and into the air or wherever it goes. Just so long as it isn't hidden anymore. We can't pretend this part of us doesn't exist." Harbor took a deep breath and then pressed on. "It's just like you told me, Ruby. With the gullsbane. You needed to make it small so it couldn't hurt anyone. If we hide it, we make it stronger. If we let it go into the light, we take away its power."

Her aunts exchanged looks. Harbor wasn't finished. "Benspeir needs to tell the truth. They can't hide it anymore. The royal line needs to tell their people that they weren't the saviors. They were the ones who brought on the violence in the first place. We need to claim our part as well. The women of Lapistyr, you hid it—*we* hid the truth."

It all made sense in Harbor's head. They'd said it was energy or like a spore or a trapped animal, but Harbor knew it was something else, something like those, but also something else entirely. Harbor also knew that anything contained hardened and that secrets often snapped. "We can't keep burying it. The past always comes back. We can't hide from it. We need to have it out in the open." She took another deep breath. "We can't destroy it. We have to face it."

There was silence among the women. Harbor hoped they would see. For so long the truth had been buried. Her father's kingdom had tried to hide their past sins, and her mother's people had helped. They couldn't hide it anymore.

Coralie stepped forward. She crouched in front of her daughter and placed her hands on Harbor's cheeks. "You are a brave girl," she said. "All these years I have strived to protect you. I have thought of little else. I wanted to shield you from all harm, all sadness, all anger, all danger. But still, somehow, when the danger came, you were able to face it."

Harbor's stomach sank. This felt like a buttering up. Her mother was saying all these kind things only to tell her that she was wrong. Harbor turned to Peter, to Anna. They understood. They had to!

Coralie stood. She grasped Harbor's hand. "My daughter, the princess, has spoken. She has spoken a hard truth that we do not want to hear." The queen's face was dirty, her hair a mess, but she looked more regal and powerful than Harbor had ever seen her.

"We will do as Princess Harbor Rose says. We will let The Frost go. We will tell the truth of our part in this story."

There was some murmuring, but no one objected.

Sapphire stood before Harbor. She placed her hand on Harbor's forehead. "May I see your vision?" she asked.

Harbor nodded and closed her eyes.

"Wait!"

Surprised by the yell, Harbor blinked open her eyes.

Standing at the edge of the fort was Micah with her wolf.

CHAPTER FORTY-TWO

Micah crossed the space between herself and the other women of Lapistyr. Her wolf stayed right at her side. They sidestepped bodies and puddles.

When Micah reached her sisters, Harbor made space for her. The wolf trotted over and sat next to Peter and Frank. The wolf sniffed Frank's face and gave it a lick.

Harbor slipped her hand into Micah's. Micah held out her hand to Sapphire. Sapphire did not take it. "With all of us, we should be strong enough to meet Harbor's will," Micah said. "It is not so simple as letting it wash away. Letting go can be as hard as trapping."

Queen Coralie looked at her sister. "You foresaw this?"

Micah shook her head. "Sapphire has the gift of foresight. I *predicted*. I have spent more time with anger and fear."

Harbor watched the women's faces. Sapphire's was as tight as a locked box. Opal Pearl looked pained. Ruby's expression was filled with pity and Amethyst's with longing. Her mother, though, cocked her head to the side. "We were not always kind to you. Even before."

Micah winced. "I had dreams that you did not. There were things I wished to know about that you did not." She glanced at Amethyst. "Most of you." She reached her hand to Sapphire again. "Such is the way of families, is it not?"

Coralie lowered her head. "If we had only listened, this day might never have come."

"So long as that danger was buried, ignored, and forgotten, this day would have come. Thanks to you, there was someone who could see how to fix it." Micah looked at Harbor. "That was my blessing for her: to save this realm—or it would have been had I not been interrupted. Luckily, Amethyst blessed her with heroism." Micah smiled at her sister. "But Harbor Rose would not have been able to fulfill that blessing without the teaching you all gave her. She would not have been able to see what needed to be done if she had not come to this island and met the people here. Or these other children. We think we can control the energy with our magic, but magic is not enough. It never is."

Coralie stepped closer to Micah. She squeezed her sister close. "You have my sincere apologies."

"Time is running short," Micah said. She reached her hand out a third time to Sapphire.

Sapphire took her sister's outstretched hand. "Your balance will temper our magic," she said.

Sapphire stood again in front of Harbor, hand on her forehead. "May I see your vision?"

Harbor closed her eyes. She pictured The Frost flying like dandelion seeds, losing all its power as it went. The flakes in her mind gained color as they dispersed, a rainbow swirl for all the people who had been lost. She blinked open her eyes.

Sapphire brought Harbor to Opal Pearl. Opal Pearl touched Harbor's arm, then nodded. She reached out both hands. She hummed, and The Frost flakes began to dance in the sky like snowflakes.

Sapphire next brought Harbor to touch Ruby's shoulder. Ruby spun her hands at the sky. A wind picked up.

Next, Sapphire brought Harbor to Amethyst. Amethyst saw Harbor's vision the most clearly. She stole the sparkle from the flakes, turned them into dull dust motes.

Harbor and Sapphire went next to Micah. She held out both hands, and Harbor placed hers on top of her aunt's. The Frost spread out wider and wider.

Finally, Harbor and Sapphire reached Queen Coralie. Coralie hugged Harbor tight, and then, still with her body pressed against Harbor's, she swirled her hands. She conjured love and fear, shame and pride, honor and jingoism— all the feelings that went along with the story of the people of Benspeir.

The circle closed itself. The sisters began speaking their words. The words tumbled together, then found a rhythm like a song. Harbor didn't understand the words, but she felt the energy move through them and through her. It was warm in her chest and cold on her skin, a million things at once. She felt it move all around them. Peter and Anna felt it, too. As did Frank, the first islander to awake. Micah's wolf howled at the clouds.

The waspgulls took to the sky. They spun upward, then fanned out over the island. Then, all at once, they flew away.

It was the last time the waspgulls were ever seen on Small Island.

CHAPTER FORTY-THREE

The sun started to peek out from among the clouds, and, as the sun set, the sky turned pink.

"Like cotton candy," Anna said. "We have skies like this back at home."

"It is the sky of better days coming," Amethyst said.

The Frost had been set free, and the islanders had woken, each in their turn. They had been confused, lost. Some had memories of what had happened; some had none. The sisters of Lapistyr were tired, but they still had magic to do. "Come, children," Ruby said. "The time is drawing long, and the door may close. We need to get you home."

"The door can close?" Anna asked.

"Oh, yes, child," Ruby said.

"The time shifts are the problem," Amethyst said. "We can put you back where you were, but if too much time passes here, the line of time marches too far past in your realm."

Ruby patted her on the head. "But cheer up. You've only been here a matter of days. There is still time."

"What's it like?" Anna asked. "Going back?"

"Like a dream," Peter said. "You wake up and there you are, right back where you were, but all groggy. And you're not sure if this is real or not. But it's real. It's very real, and now we both know."

They all walked together down to the sea. The rocks were slippery and covered in barnacles. The children walked with their hands out to the side like tightrope walkers, but the sisters seemed to glide along the tops of the rocks. With Micah with them, their full strength had returned. They were whole again.

When they came to where the waves lapped at the rocks, they were all silent for a while. Harbor could feel the grief already starting to pour over her. "Will you come back?" she asked Peter.

"Of course I will. We're true-blue friends forever. We made a pinky promise. You can call me back whenever you need me. Or, you know, just because."

Ruby said, "Oh, but you can't come back."

"You've been here three times, Peter," Amethyst said. "We can only send you back three times. If you came again, you'd have to stay."

"Forever?" Anna asked.

"Forever," Opal Pearl confirmed.

"But you could come again, Anna. If you see the door," Ruby said.

Harbor and Peter stared at each other and then looked away. Harbor's heart ached. She wanted to grab hold of him, tell him to stay. But she knew she could not do that—could not ask him to give up his family and his life the way that she had lost hers. She threw her arms around him tightly. "I will miss you so very much!" she said. "You're the best friend I've ever had."

"I'm the only friend you've ever had."

Harbor shook her head against his shoulder. "I was so selfish," she said. "If I hadn't wanted you to come to play with me, then we might have more time. Future time."

"I wanted to come," he said. "Anyway, who knows how old I would be if you could call me back. I might be a boring old adult."

Harbor pulled back from him and looked him right in the eyes. "You are a hero, Peter," she told him. "No matter what that Cam person says. Or your father. Or most of all, you. Without you, all my people would still be locked away in their own bodies by The Frost. You saved them. You and Anna." Her voice cracked. "Never forget that you are a true hero, in any realm."

"Thank you," Peter said. He didn't know what else to say to her.

He took Anna's hand, and together they walked into the sea. Peter had done this twice before, but there was a hint of fear on Anna's face.

"Hero," Harbor said to him.

The sisters made a circle of their hands and tilted their

heads to the center. The words they spoke were in an old language, quiet and run together. The words washed over and through Harbor, like waves. Then, Peter and Anna slipped under the water and were gone, back to Kansas.

Harbor collapsed in a heap and cried.

The aunts circled around her. They leaned in and covered her with their bodies. Together they wept. They wept for Peter and Anna. They wept for years lost. They wept for what they still had to face. The Frost had gone, but the past remained. When their weeping was done, the sisters fell away from one another. "There are things you need to know," Sapphire said.

"The other village? And shifting the island?" Harbor asked. "Mr. Coffin said you moved the island from the other realm to this one, but—"

Amethyst held up her hands. "Slow down, child," she said. "There is much to know and plenty of time to know it."

"We didn't move the island, precisely," Opal Pearl conceded. "But we needed it empty. We couldn't risk people stumbling upon the thin places. We invited the islanders to our realm. Some stayed. Some chose not to. They were well compensated either way."

"We hid the island in the other realm. In Peter and Anna's realm, that is. It was still there, but hidden," Sapphire explained. "It might as well only exist here."

"We chose the larger of the two villages to live in; the one safer from storms—and attack," Opal Pearl said.

"The lighthouse could serve as a watchtower," Sapphire added.

On and on, they explained the island to her. It was always meant to keep her safe.

Harbor stood on her boulder. She looked in the direction of Kansas, or where she thought it might be. She remembered each moment with Peter and Anna. Never once did those two hesitate. They were ready to follow her into whatever might come. She wasn't sure she would ever have friends like that again.

She crouched down onto the rock and tasted the salt spray on her lips. Small Island had always caught her, always protected her, it was true. Maybe, though, that time was over. Maybe it was time for a princess to brave the unprotected world.

CHAPTER FORTY-FOUR

The sun was rising in a clear blue sky. Mr. Coffin and Harbor stood in the water to their ankles, but they were not beachcombing. They were saying goodbye.

Frank stood on the beach, hands in his pockets. His hair had gone back to chocolate brown except for one small patch of white.

"If you toss a bottle into the sea, it will wash up here," Mr. Coffin said. "I am sure of it."

"And you will toss one back?" she asked.

"Absolutely."

Frank stepped closer. "I'm going to need that figure back now, Harbor girl. The one I made of you."

Harbor handed the figure to him. Frank handed it to Mr. Coffin saying, "You'll find a whole set back in your shop—all the aunts and the Murphys and the king and the queen. A regular hand-carved chess set."

Frank smiled. "And so we don't miss them too much, I made us one, too."

He handed her a wooden box that he had at his feet. She opened it, and resting in velvet inside were wooden figures of each of the islanders: the Templetons, Mr. Coffin, Mr. Broom, Ada Flynn. Where the king and queen should be were Peter and Anna.

Harbor hugged him. "It's the most wonderful gift I've ever received."

They were all three crying. Harbor squeezed Mr. Coffin tight. He kissed the top of her head. Then Frank reached out his hand to her. "We have a mighty journey ahead of us."

Harbor had asked Frank to come with her. She knew she could trust him above anyone else. "Are you frightened?" she asked him.

"Yes," he said. "But I won't let that stop me this time."

They walked together down to the dock where all the villagers stood waiting.

Mr. Broom was all patched up but walked with a cane now. Frank had carved it for him. "You keep an eye out for elephants, my island girl," he said to her.

Mary Templeton handed her a basket full of blueberry cornbread. Hod told her to keep her wits about her. Ada Flynn gave her a stack of aprons, each with half a dozen pockets.

Frank and Harbor stopped next to her mother. There was a skiff waiting for them. The others—the sisters and the

Murphys—were already on the large Lapistyr ship that had brought the soldiers.

Mr. Coffin crouched down in front of Harbor. "You *are* an island girl, Princess Harbor Rose. You're our princess, as well as theirs, and don't you ever forget it."

Harbor smiled through her tears. "I won't, Mr. Coffin. I promise."

Frank got in the skiff first and held out his hand to the queen. She took her seat at the bow. Harbor climbed in and took a seat at the oars.

"Is that how it is now?" Frank asked.

"Yes," Harbor said.

He took a seat beside her, and together they started rowing.

She was a princess of two realms. She was going home. She was leaving home. An ending and a beginning, all in one, with the ocean stretched out in front of her. The water glittered. The horizon beckoned. Harbor Rose was ready to set sail.

ACKNOWLEDGMENTS

Over two decades before the writing of this book, a child was born. She was the daughter of my best friend. A group of women, friends since childhood, arrived at the house to meet the new baby. It felt to me like Sleeping Beauty's fairy godmothers coming to grant blessings, and, since then, I've wanted to write a book about a girl and her aunties. So, thank you to Sophia for calling the aunties into existence, and thank you to the aunties—Larissa Crockett, Sarah Newkirk, Jessie Forbes, and Lindsay Oakes—for all the support, advice, and friendship over the years.

This book is set to release on my brother's birthday, and so it seems important to thank Matt Frazer for being my first co-writer in the world of make-believe.

Thank you to my dad, Joseph Frazer, for sharing his love of the sea with me. Thank you to Dad and Susan Tananbaum for taking our family out to all the Maine islands that inspired this story.

My mom, Eileen Frazer, is the greatest champion and has supported me every day of my life. Thank you, thank you, thank you.

I am lucky to have wonderful in-laws who come at the drop of a hat so that I can write, travel, and, frankly, get some sleep. Ed and Audrey Blakemore, you are the best!

Thank you to Sara Crowe for guiding me through the rough seas and frightening tunnels of the publishing world. Thank you as well to everyone at Pippin Properties. I am so grateful to have found a literary home with you.

Mary Kate Castellani, you are the best editor a writer could hope for. When I don't know how to fix an issue, I know you will ask just the right question or offer just enough advice so I can see the solution. Thank you for pushing me to up the magic in this story. Your advice is truly a blessing.

Thank you to the whole team at Bloomsbury: Beth Eller, Ariana Abad, Kei Nakatsuka, Rebecca McGlynn, Laura Phillips, Donna Mark, Yelena Safronova, Erica Barmash, Lily Yengle, Phoebe Dyer, Faye Bi, Alona Fryman, Erica Chan, and Kathleen Morandini.

Khoa Le, thank you for your beautiful artwork for the cover of this book. It takes my breath away.

Finally, as always, thank you to my husband, Nathan, and my kids, Jack and Matilda, for everything. You are the people I most want to adventure with, in this realm and in all the others, too.